"Than**ks** ~~for your com~~**pany,**" Matt sa~~id.~~

"You're welcome," Caroline replied. "Thanks for being my victim in the self-defense class tonight. Virginia said she'd find some extra volunteers for the other nights, so you don't have to come. Unless you want to."

Did he want to? Matt hadn't made a fool of himself over a girl in a long time. There were a few relationships in college, and even though one of them had lasted an entire semester, he was quite sure he hadn't felt the emotional roller coaster Caroline put him on.

The smart choice would be to cut a wide swath around her.

"I'll see what my schedule looks like."

Caroline put a hand on the door lever, but then turned to him and paused, lips slightly parted. Had she not been a police officer with a powerful curiosity about an incident involving his family, he might have leaned forward and kissed her.

But that was a risk he was not ready to take.

Dear Reader,

Thank you for visiting my summer resort and amusement park, Starlight Point, as you read *Until the Ride Stops*. This is the fourth book of Starlight Point Stories, which also includes *Under the Boardwalk*, *Carousel Nights* and *Meet Me on the Midway*. In the first three books, the Hamilton siblings take ownership of Starlight Point and find true love. Readers met Scott Bennett in *Meet Me on the Midway*, when he and Evie Hamilton have a summer romance. Scott's younger sister, Caroline, has a roller-coaster affair of her own in *Until the Ride Stops* as she spends her second summer on the Starlight Point Police Department digging into a cold case that could destroy the man she loves.

I hope you'll love this book, and also visit me at amiedenman.com, follow me on Twitter at @amiedenman or send me an email at author@amiedenman.com.

Best wishes!

Amie Denman

HEARTWARMING

Until the Ride Stops

———

Amie Denman

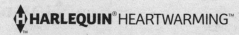
HARLEQUIN® HEARTWARMING™

Recycling programs
for this product may
not exist in your area.

ISBN-13: 978-0-373-36856-3

Until the Ride Stops

Copyright © 2017 by Amie Denman

All rights reserved. Except for use in any review, the reproduction or utilization of this work in whole or in part in any form by any electronic, mechanical or other means, now known or hereinafter invented, including xerography, photocopying and recording, or in any information storage or retrieval system, is forbidden without the written permission of the publisher, Harlequin Enterprises Limited, 225 Duncan Mill Road, Don Mills, Ontario M3B 3K9, Canada.

This is a work of fiction. Names, characters, places and incidents are either the product of the author's imagination or are used fictitiously, and any resemblance to actual persons, living or dead, business establishments, events or locales is entirely coincidental.

This edition published by arrangement with Harlequin Books S.A.

For questions and comments about the quality of this book, please contact us at CustomerService@Harlequin.com.

® and TM are trademarks of Harlequin Enterprises Limited or its corporate affiliates. Trademarks indicated with ® are registered in the United States Patent and Trademark Office, the Canadian Intellectual Property Office and in other countries.

Printed in U.S.A.

Amie Denman is the author of a dozen contemporary romances full of humor and heart. Born with an overdeveloped sense of curiosity, she's been known to chase fire trucks on her bicycle and eavesdrop on lovers' conversations. Amie lives in Ohio with her husband, two sons, a big yellow Labrador and two cats. She believes everything is fun, especially wedding cake, show tunes, roller coasters and falling in love.

Books by Amie Denman

Harlequin Heartwarming

Starlight Point Stories

Under the Boardwalk
Carousel Nights
Meet Me on the Midway

Carina Press

Her Lucky Catch

Visit the Author Profile page at Harlequin.com for more titles.

To my best friend and writing critique partner, May Williams. Thank you for your brains, your talent, your patience and your friendship. I would be nowhere without you.

CHAPTER ONE

CAROLINE BENNETT CREPT into the police chief's office and pulled the chain on the light bulb hanging over the rusty filing cabinets in the corner. She booted up the laptop and pushed the power button on the document scanner she'd borrowed from the Starlight Point IT department. All the usual sounds of the amusement park—yells of excitement, midway games and the roar of roller coasters—were eerily absent late at night and the quiet added to the sensation she was doing something wrong.

She pulled open the top drawer labeled 1970–1973. Hanging file folders were labeled by month and year, with bits of paper sticking out of some. She took out the January 1970 folder and placed its single yellowed paper on the scanner's glass.

While she waited for the blue light to capture the document, she slid open the bottom drawer and took out the July 1985 folder. Caroline glanced over her shoulder before opening it.

She found several smaller manila folders labeled Employee Issues, Dispatcher's Log, Misdemeanors. The fourth folder was labeled Loose Cannon. She opened it and discovered it was completely empty.

"Caroline."

She jumped and turned to the door.

"Sorry," the night dispatcher said. "I thought I'd just walk in here and tell you instead of putting it over the radio."

"That's okay," Caroline said. She took a deep breath, trying to calm her racing heart. "Is there a call?"

"One of the night cleaners reported seeing a possible trespasser enter the construction zone for the new ride."

"I'll go right over," Caroline said. She shoved the July 1985 folder back into the drawer and closed it.

"Want me to scan some of this old stuff? Nothing's more boring than night shift. Nothing ever happens."

"No," Caroline said quickly. She smiled and tried to sound appreciative. "It's my way of trying to get on the chief's good side so he'll recommend me for the police academy this fall."

"If you make it through all that old crap," the dispatcher said, nodding at the filing cabinets, "you'll deserve a badge."

Caroline shut down the scanner and laptop and sped out the door.

She crossed the midway, a wide avenue lined with shops and food stands on both sides, and checked the gate in the fence surrounding the construction area. Still locked. That meant the trespasser must have entered through one of the other four gates.

The new ride wouldn't open for almost a year, and there was no spectacular coaster track visible, but management wanted to protect the construction site. Crews were busy leveling and stabilizing the ground, pouring concrete footers and laying the groundwork for the first new ride Starlight Point had built in three years.

And it would be a doozy. A combined kiddie coaster looping in and out of the track of a high-speed thrill coaster. Something for everyone, but still top secret until the big media reveal planned for later in the summer.

"Hold it right there," she said. The words were out of her mouth before she'd even focused on the moving shadow in front of her. "Hands where I can see them."

She pulled a flashlight off her belt and lit up the suspect. The suspect's back. He wore loose fitting jeans, a T-shirt and a hard hat.

A hard hat? Not many trespassers donned safety equipment. If he was a worker on the site, what was he doing there at midnight?

"Don't shoot," the man said. "The only thing I have on me is a cell phone and a case of insomnia."

"What are you doing here?"

"Worrying," he said.

"You're in a restricted area. You'll have to worry somewhere else. I need to ask you to come with me."

The man turned around, hands in the air, and faced Caroline. She kept her flashlight on him, even though he didn't look dangerous. He had a blond crew cut and a big smile. Broad shoulders. Exposed biceps with his hands in the air. "You got coffee where we're going?"

"This isn't a coffee break. I'm arresting you."

"Can you do that?" he asked.

"Of course I can," she said. Irritation tightened the muscles in her jaw. "I'm a member of the Starlight Point Police Department."

He laughed and put his hands down. "I didn't mean to challenge your authority. I just wondered if you made a habit of arresting people who are legitimately working."

"At midnight?"

He shrugged. "Job never rests."

Caroline lowered her flashlight so it wasn't hitting him square in the face. "Explain yourself."

"Formal greeting first," he said. He held out his hand, but Caroline didn't take it. "Matt Dunbar. Construction engineer on the Super Star and Shooting Star project."

"Shh," Caroline said, looking around. "You're not supposed to use the official name. Someone might hear."

"Sorry," he said. He leaned closer and whispered, "Matt Dunbar, construction engineer on the nameless mystery project opening next May. I hope."

Caroline let her shoulders relax but didn't let down her guard. He still hadn't explained himself. Not really, anyway.

"That's enough," Caroline said. "Tell me why you're here at midnight. I don't see any of your crew, and I didn't think there was nighttime construction going on."

"Couldn't sleep, so I walked over." He gave up on the handshake and put both hands in his pockets.

"Walked?"

Starlight Point was on a peninsula jutting into Lake Huron with a long bridge providing nearly the only access. No one walked to Starlight Point. They either caught the ferry or drove over. Caroline narrowed her eyes. His story was not holding water so far.

"From the campout. My company sponsored a tent and I drew one of the lucky tickets to stay over tonight."

Of course Caroline knew about the campout. It was the reason she was working an overnight shift. With a five-hundred-dollar donation to a local charity, groups of four could pitch a tent and stay on the Western Trail overnight. They'd get VIP treatment when the park opened in the morning.

"You're here for the coaster campout?"

"It sounded like a good idea at the time.

Stay the night, campfire breakfast and coasters at first light before the crowds get here. Nice donation to local charities. However, I forgot two things."

"What did you forget?" Perhaps this would explain why he was wandering the construction zone. Caroline was still considering whether or not to haul him over to the station where she could question him under harsh fluorescent lights. Protecting Starlight Point was not a joke to her.

"I don't like riding roller coasters."

"And yet you're building one," Caroline said. She was starting to doubt he was actually in charge of the project. Shouldn't it be someone much older? She'd been patrolling the fence surrounding the high-profile construction for several weeks now, but she'd hardly noticed the men in hard hats coming and going. "Will you ride this coaster when it's done?"

He nodded, his expression serious in the ambient glow from the flashlight. "It's my job. Inspires confidence if the man who builds it is willing to ride it. Even if I have to hold my breath for the entire ride."

"Dedication," Caroline said. *I can respect that.* But something still did not add up.

"You said there were two things. What else did you forget?" Caroline asked. "Is it here in the construction zone?"

"No. It's a fact—I hate camping. When I was a kid, my older cousins used to consider it a badge of honor to scare me to death by scratching on the outside of the tent like ravenous mountain lions. This was especially effective after ghost stories and urban legends around the campfire."

Caroline suppressed a laugh. "I'm Caroline Bennett," she said, holding out her hand. "I went camping one time when I was a Girl Scout."

"And?"

"I was trapped in a tent with a spider large enough to cast a shadow."

He took her hand and gave it a lingering shake. "I'm picturing you ordering the spider out of your tent. Or else."

She smiled. "The spider disappeared and we never found it, even though we stayed up all night looking."

"I have no doubt you're braver than I am," he said. "Which is why I've already decided to surrender should you cuff me and haul me off to the Starlight Point Jail. I just hope you serve funnel cakes and boardwalk fries for breakfast. It's the least you could do for keeping a man from his own worries."

"What are you worried about?"

"Getting this done in the next three hundred and forty-two days."

Caroline pulled her radio off her belt and keyed the police dispatcher to let her know the situation was under control and she would be escorting a guest back to the camping area. She clipped the radio to her belt and gave Matt her attention again.

"So you wandered off the Western Trail and thought you'd poke around here since you couldn't sleep?"

A line appeared between his eyebrows as he scanned the area. "I just thought it might be interesting to get the lay of the land at night. I'm trying to picture it all lit up with miles of steel track going everywhere."

Caroline glanced around. It was dark inside the walled-off section of the park, especially after closing time when lights all over the Point were dimmed or switched off.

Only the chasing lights on the tall hills of a few roller coasters were visible.

By next season, there would be an addition to the Starlight Point skyline. The new top secret coaster was being built on the site of the ill-fated and short-lived Loose Cannon that had claimed a life and closed after only part of one season.

She shuddered, imagining the girl being thrown from the ride and dying on what should have been a fun day.

"Cold?" Matt asked.

Caroline shook her head. No way was she sharing her plan to investigate an old case no one wanted to reopen.

"I wish I had a jacket to offer you," he said. "I could give you my hard hat but it won't do much good."

"I should escort you out of here and secure the site," Caroline said. She swung her flashlight in an arc toward the gate. "Let's go. I'll see you back to your tent."

Matt blew out a long breath. Maybe he wanted to stay and work, but she couldn't allow it. It was her job to keep the area free of trespassers all night. No matter what they claimed. She planned to check his name and credentials the next morning.

"Will you come in and do a spider check?" he asked.

She pressed her lips together to suppress a smile. "You'll have to handle that yourself. Not in my job description."

Caroline opened the gate and they walked onto the dimly lit, empty midway. During the day, there was barely room for a shadow on the crowded thoroughfare, and now it was abandoned.

Matt fell into step beside her as they passed the long fence concealing the construction site and then the dodgem cars and several shuttered food stands. The late May evening was chilly and the damp air smelled like the earth recently churned up in the flowerbeds. A lingering aroma of hot dogs and fried food remained, even hours after park closing.

"Have you worked here long?" Matt asked.

"This is my second season," she said, hoping the finality in her tone would discourage him from asking further questions. If she hurried back to the station, she could reclaim the second half of her lunch break and get another look at that file. Was it really empty or had the contents been misfiled?

"So you want to be a police officer, huh?"

"I am a police officer," she said. "I'm a member of the Starlight Point Police Department."

"But you don't have a gun."

She shot him a sideways look and squared her shoulders. Was he planning to challenge her? He'd find out she could take down a man his size before he saw it coming.

He laughed. "Easy, sergeant. It was just an observation."

"I'm not a sergeant. And I don't carry a gun yet," she said. "I plan to complete the police academy over the next year."

"Then I better watch out," he said. "Or at least stay in my tent at night."

They passed the loading platform for the cable cars, Tosha's Homemade Ice Cream and the scrambler ride. Caroline began to wonder why she'd offered to escort him all the way to his tent like a lost kid. Maybe she should just point him in the right direction.

She could tell him she'd be watching him and he would probably comply.

But it was a quiet night. And walking under the stars was pleasant. And she was completing the trespassing call she'd answered by making certain the perpetrator was secured for the night. She could zip up his tent and wash her hands of him.

"Too bad none of the vendors are open," he said. "I'd like to buy you a soda to thank you for walking me home down the mean streets of Starlight Point."

"You're not in danger," she said.

"I can't see in the dark," he replied. "I could fall and break both elbows, and then the new ride would be behind schedule."

"Hard to believe you can't manage in the dark when you wandered all the way to the construction site without a flashlight."

He stopped, faced her and smiled. "You got me. How about taking a lap around the peninsula?"

"No."

"It might tire me out and cure my insomnia. Then you'll know I'm snoring away in my tent the rest of the night."

Caroline pointed down the Western Trail and started walking again. "Not negotiable. I'm depositing you in the camping zone where one of my colleagues is on guard. I'll have Big Kenny keep an eye on you."

Matt sighed. "You're no fun."

"Not in my job description."

They crossed the train tracks where an old-fashioned steam engine chugged past dozens of times every day, pulling passengers through a shoot-out with animatronic characters in a Western ghost town. Caroline enjoyed a mellow trip around Starlight Point in the open train cars on days when her feet were tired or she wanted to unwind, but most days she preferred buckling in for a heart-stopping ride on the roller coasters Starlight Point was beginning to be known for.

"I love roller coasters," she said aloud. "And I'm still curious why a guy who builds them doesn't."

"I don't just build roller coasters. I'm a construction engineer, which means I build whatever's on the blueprints. I've built everything from playgrounds to senior citizen housing. This summer and winter, my job's a roller coaster. I make sure it gets done correctly and on time."

"Which is why you have insomnia," she observed.

"Exactly. At this stage of the game, it's like being in an abstract painting. And I think it's only going to get worse."

As they made their way along the Western Trail, they started seeing tents.

Matt stopped and whispered, "This is my tent. I think. They all look alike."

"Oh," Caroline said. She was almost disappointed. Of all the things she'd thought might happen during the overnight campout, she hadn't expected a pleasant stroll under the stars with a mislabeled trespasser who built rides he didn't plan to enjoy. He was charming, but she wished she hadn't had to surrender the Loose Cannon folder as soon as she'd finally gotten her hands on it.

"Good night, then," she said.

He smiled and leaned too close. "You're going to stand here and make sure I go inside, aren't you?"

"Just watching out for lions," she said. She crossed her arms and watched him slide the zipper up and quietly crawl through the opening. As she walked away, she paused a moment and scratched on the slippery nylon tent.

CHAPTER TWO

MATT DUNBAR SHADED his eyes and peered through the surveyor's scope. The project was massive. And unique. Mixing a kiddie coaster with an adult coaster could be genius. Or a total flop. Would little kids line up for a ride that looked scary even if it wasn't?

That wasn't his problem. Starlight Point knew its customers better than he did. His responsibility was to make sure the intertwined coasters were built according to the blueprints, the code, the budget and the calendar.

One year. The ride had to open next May, and it had to be perfect. Perfection in a roller coaster meant it had to seem deadly when in reality, riders wouldn't break a fingernail. He shook his head. Such a paradox.

Millions of dollars were on the line, as well as his company's reputation and his own hopes and dreams. He had to prove himself. Not many twenty-six-year-olds got an opportunity like this. The media attention at the groundbreaking ceremony a few weeks ago was enough to remind him how high profile Starlight Point was. He'd seen his own picture on the front page of the *Bayside Times* with a caption saying the top secret project was all on him. *Great.*

Matt looked up when something caught his eye across the construction zone. A tall man, suit coat flapping, made his way over the mud and around the equipment.

Jack Hamilton. He and his sisters, Evie and June, were co-owners of Starlight Point. He was a nice enough guy and they had something in common—Jack had inherited the park from his parents, much like Matt believed he might inherit Bayside Construction someday. Perhaps sooner than he'd ever thought. His chest tightened when he thought of his stepfather's declining health.

"How's it going?" Jack asked.

"Good," Matt said. He shoved his hard hat back and wiped sweat from his brow. "This part of the project isn't much to look at, but it's necessary. Even though it seems like we're just making a mess."

"I remember when the Sea Devil site looked like this four years ago. I had a hard time picturing it ever becoming a ride. My sisters still claim I don't have any imagination, but the problem is usually just that I'm hungry. Want to get a doughnut?"

Matt glanced at his watch. He'd been on-site for three hours now and the midmorning belly rumble was slowing him down. "I could eat a doughnut."

Jack slapped him on the back. "Let's go to the bakery just down the midway. But you might want to take off your hard hat so you don't attract attention. The park's open, and people are dying of curiosity because of this fence. Of course, it's our strategy to build excitement and that's why we swore your company to secrecy."

"Is the strategy working?"

"I get media requests for details and the ride name every day. And our police department has already chased at least one trespasser out of here, so I'd say yes," Jack said.

Jack's face betrayed nothing, and as far as Matt knew, Jack wasn't talking about him.

"Gawkers," Matt said.

Jack shrugged. "It's a pain, but I'm glad

people are excited about the ride. It's a huge investment for us and we could lose our shirts if it fails." He grinned. "No pressure or anything."

Matt followed Jack through the mud zone to a gate partially obscured by a tree. He hung his yellow hard hat on a nail before he left the construction area.

"Pink awning," Jack said, inclining his head down the midway. "Land of sweets."

Matt didn't see a pink awning. He saw a tall, slim police officer all in black. She stood, shoulders squared, watching the crowd. Her posture said *don't mess with me*.

It was too much temptation. As he and Jack neared Caroline, Matt stopped.

"Excuse me, miss. Can you tell me what they're building?" He pointed toward the long fence around the coaster project.

Caroline crossed her arms and cocked her head. *She recognizes me for certain.*

"They're building a swinging bridge that will connect Starlight Point to the mainland," she said with straight lips and a professional tone. "It will be the longest bridge built from licorice in North America."

"That's what I heard," Matt said. "I'll be sure to spread the word on social media."

Jack laughed. "We're getting doughnuts, Caroline. You want one?"

The owner knows her first name and is offering her doughnuts? Matt glanced at her silver name tag which only displayed her last name. Bennett.

"Of course I do," Caroline said. "Cinnamon roll. Maple frosting. I have a break coming up, and I'm a lot nicer to teenagers with sugar in my bloodstream. This place is crawling with school groups."

"I'll bring two," Jack said.

Jack and Matt strode toward the far end of the midway. When they had gone a few steps, Jack grinned. "My sister-in-law," he said. "Interesting lady."

"Really?"

"Her brother, Scott, just got married to my sister Evie a few weeks ago. Caroline was a bridesmaid."

As they approached the pink awning with Aunt Augusta's Midway Bakery spelled out in script, a woman leaned across the counter. Jack gave her a quick kiss on the lips.

Matt began to feel as if he was in the twilight zone.

"My wife, Augusta," Jack said.

Matt shook hands with the dark-haired woman and turned to Jack. "Are you related to everyone here?"

Augusta drew her eyebrows together and looked at her husband.

"We just talked with Caroline," Jack explained. "She wants two cinnamon rolls."

"With maple frosting," Matt added. Augusta and Jack both turned their attention to Matt and he felt his ears get hot. *So I pay attention to detail, so what?* "Could you also box up a dozen for my crew? I can't go back there and eat in front of them unless I bring enough to share."

They ate their doughnuts while they walked back toward the construction site. Matt gave Jack the progress report, which didn't differ much from the week before. Things were moving along on schedule, but it was still early. And worrying about the project really did keep Matt awake at night.

Jack's phone rang as they passed the Kiddie Land motorcycles chasing each other on a track. He answered, listened and dropped the phone back into the pocket of his suit coat. "I need to go to my office," he said. "Will you deliver Caroline's doughnuts?"

"Sure."

Jack handed over a white pastry bag, waved and left the midway with long strides. He cut through Kiddie Land, his steps keeping time with the beeping horns and flashing lights.

Matt headed toward the long fence where Caroline stood like a post, arms crossed. He held out the bag and was gratified to see her posture relax as she reached for it with a hint of a smile.

"Thanks," she said.

"Anytime." He balanced his crew's box of doughnuts on his hip. "If you're going to be out here all summer, we should get to know each other. So far I know you don't like spiders or camping, you're merciless with a flashlight and you like pastries more than teenagers."

"Everyone likes pastries more than teenagers," Caroline said. She opened the bag and looked inside, nodding approval at what she saw.

"I can't believe you doubted me," Matt said.

"Aren't you supposed to be on the other side of the fence?"

"Yes. But I get out every now and then. Like when we're waiting for a fresh truckload of licorice."

Caroline smiled. "Sorry about that. While I'm standing here, I make up ridiculous answers to the question about what we're building, but I can't use my snarky answers with actual guests. I don't think the Hamiltons would be impressed."

"But you're related to them. Jack said your brother married his sister."

She nodded. "They met last summer."

"And Jack met his wife here, too?"

"Yes. That was before I worked here."

"Must be something in the air," Matt said.

Caroline raised her eyebrows but didn't say anything.

"You could probably have your pick of jobs with family connections like yours. Why are you standing in the hot sun warding off gawkers outside a construction zone?"

Her jaw tightened and she turned steely eyes on him. "I'm willing to work my way up and earn my stripes. Justice is a serious business."

Matt cleared his throat. "So is building stuff. I should get back to work. We're digging out some old roller coaster footers."

"From the Loose Cannon," Caroline said.

Matt bit his lip and goose bumps lifted along his back. When Bayside Construction had won the bid to build the new coaster practically on top of the one his uncle had built, he'd asked his stepfather for more information. The older man had muttered something about letting sleeping dogs lie. Bruce Corbin's heart was delicate, and Matt hadn't pushed for details.

Why was Caroline so quick with the coaster's name? She seemed to be a few years younger than he was, and the Loose Cannon was gone long before either one of them was born.

"How did you know about that?"

"I…studied a little park history. It's no secret. A roller coaster named the Loose Cannon was built on this site back in the 1980s."

Did she sound defensive?

"I'll have to come find you if I ever need a history lesson on Starlight Point," Matt said.

Caroline shifted her gaze to the side, refusing to meet his eyes.

Someone tapped him on the shoulder and he turned to find a giant man in a black uniform.

"Is this guy bothering you?" the man asked Caroline.

"No," she said. "He was asking directions." She turned and pointed to the tree that concealed the entrance gate into the construction site. "That's where you want to go."

She walked away, leaving Matt with the giant police officer.

"Guess you ought to move along," the man said. "Before she comes back and finds you hanging around."

Matt let himself through the gate, shoved his hard hat on and went back to work. He considered opening a conversation with Caroline—or anyone—about the Loose Cannon. His stepfather brushing him off had been out of character. It made Matt wonder if there was more to the brief story in the family archive of things-we-don't-talk-about. Considering his stepfamily's connection to that ride, he was tempted to find out how much Caroline knew, just to be on the safe side.

Right now, he had work to do. This project

would make or break Bayside Construction. And in the process, it would determine the fate of the people he loved most.

Caroline clocked out, changed out of her uniform and headed for the filing cabinets in the corner of her chief's office.

Some of her friends from the rides and foods departments were meeting up to play volleyball and picnic on the beach. Wasn't the wide swath of sand in front of the Lake Breeze Hotel much more inviting than musty old files?

But she had a mission. Impress her boss and get his recommendation for the limited police academy class beginning in September. Just as important, she wanted answers about the Loose Cannon roller coaster.

She'd heard the rumors last summer, and she'd been curious about what had caused the accident. Then a few weeks ago, she'd discovered that the reclusive older couple who lived down the street from her parents had lost their daughter to the accident, but they'd never gotten any answers. The scars were so deep and wide, they'd moved away from Bayside to Yorkville where Caroline had grown up.

Caroline knew what it was like to lose someone senselessly. Perhaps that's why the quiet Knights had finally shared their story with her.

She'd known them for years, stopping by their porch on her paper route, shoveling their sidewalk in the winter. She remembered walking past their house on the way to school one spring day when she was in sixth grade. Mrs. Knight had stood on the porch and stared at her sadly but kindly. "You remind me of my daughter," she'd said.

Caroline had always wondered where the daughter was, expecting her to appear out of nowhere when she dropped off misdirected mail or stopped by with cinnamon bread her mother made on snowy days.

But Jenny Knight had died, her death on the Loose Cannon ruled accidental. It was hard to believe a life could be erased like a chalk drawing with no one to blame.

Somewhere in these rusty filing cabinets, there could be answers. But to find them, she'd have to spend hours scanning all the files.

"Are you sure you want to do this on your own time?" the police chief asked. "We could work it into your shift and cover you out on the midway."

She shook her head. "It's good experience."

Chief Bert Walker sat in a roller chair and used his heels to shove the chair back and forth. "Raking leaves is good experience, but I still pay the neighbor kid to do it so I don't have to. This is a lousy job."

Caroline sent him a quick smile and opened the second drawer of the cabinet on the far left. Folders with dates ranging from 1974–1978 filled the drawer.

"Should I throw these away after I scan them?" she asked.

Walker shrugged. "Seems like it would be safe to do that, but you never know when someone's going to want to see the real thing. And these are actual public and criminal records."

Caroline's heart thumped in her chest. "Do people request old records very often?"

"No. Big city departments, maybe. But not here, not in years. Especially not records from before you were born."

She pulled out the first folder in the drawer and turned on the scanner. "Am I going to find anything interesting in here?"

The chief rolled back and forth in his chair, watching as she carefully laid papers inside the marked area on the scanner glass. She closed the lid, pressed a button and a blue streak of light slid out.

"Probably not," Walker said. "In my career here, I've only seen a few things that would make it onto the evening news."

"Such as?"

"Rash of car thefts in the 1990s, right from the parking lot. People stole cars and stereos."

"Pretty bold."

"They were," the chief agreed. "That's why we have the tower in the parking lot. Used to be the worst job sitting in that tower watching the cars."

"Worse than scanning all these files?"

"Tough call." He leaned back in his chair. "We also had some fights over the years, some of them ugly like the one last summer, but you already knew about that one 'cause you were there. Employee theft from cash registers," he continued, "thefts in the dorms or the hotel. But quiet for the most part. I've had years' worth of petty stuff and general peace."

"When was your first summer?" Caroline asked.

"1985."

Her heart flipped again. "You've been the chief that long?"

He laughed. "No. I started out just like you. Nonbond without a gun for a few summers, then the academy, then bonded officer for a few years before I moved up the chain."

"Wasn't 1985 the year of the accident on the Loose Cannon?" she asked, trying for a casual tone. This was the opportunity she'd been waiting for, a chance to bring up the old case with someone who was there. Who better than a police officer?

The chief spun his chair around so she couldn't see his face when he said, "Yes."

"And you were a nonbond?"

"I was."

He completed the spin and met her eyes. "That was a real shame."

"The accident?"

"All of it," he said.

"Were you part of the investigation?"

He shook his head. "No. I was low man in the pecking order. And ride accident falls under the state anyway. They came out and did the inspection, wrote it up."

"Did they find out what caused the accident?"

He scratched his head.

She waited.

Jenny Knight's parents had already told her it was ruled as undetermined. But Caroline didn't want to show her hand. She was more interested in hearing what he knew.

"It was an accident, they said. Sometimes you never know exactly what goes on."

Caroline slid the paper off the scanner, replaced it in the folder and put it back in the drawer. She took out the next folder, marked February 1974, and began scanning the thin file of documents.

Chief Walker got up abruptly and his chair rolled into the wall with a solid clunk. "Happened a long time ago."

Caroline finished the February folder quickly. *Not much action in the winter.*

"The Loose Cannon was in the same place the new ride's going, wasn't it?" she asked, as if she were just killing time with conversation. "It'll be nice to have something fun there instead of just concrete and benches."

The chief grunted. "You seem awfully interested in this," he said.

She smiled at him, trying to make her curiosity seem innocent. "I want to be an investigator someday. I have to practice asking questions."

"And learn when it's best to stop," the chief said. He shuffled out to the dispatcher's desk, said something to the officer on duty and left the station.

Caroline watched him leave and wondered how many questions she should risk asking. Was he right about learning when to stop? Or was he issuing a warning?

CHAPTER THREE

TRAFFIC DUTY. Not her favorite. There was no shade on the Point Bridge. There was no end in sight to the line of cars flowing across the bridge for a Saturday in the park. And why couldn't people understand how to follow the orange traffic cones? Was it rocket science?

Last summer, she'd watched her partner bounce off the hood of a car whose driver wasn't paying attention. That was an experience she'd never forget. Or repeat.

Caroline kept her eyes on the incoming cars, their drivers distracted by digging through purses and wallets for the parking fee or for their season pass. One more hour and she could hand this job to someone else and take up her post along the midway where she usually guarded the construction zone. A shade tree with her name on it was waiting for her.

A heavy-duty pickup truck, loud diesel engine rumbling, pulled up in front of Caroline's post near the tollbooth. The driver cut the engine. What was he doing? There was a line of cars a mile long behind him and he was blocking an entire lane.

She tried to give him the move-it-along look she'd been practicing, but bright morning sun reflected off his window and she couldn't see his face.

The window slid down a moment later and Matt Dunbar rested his elbow on the frame.

"What are you doing out here?" he asked. "I can't work unless I know you're outside my construction fence keeping me safe."

"I don't always work in that zone," she said. "Nobody likes traffic duty, so we have to take turns." She approached his truck so she wouldn't have to shout over the traffic noise. "You have to move along. You're blocking a lane."

Matt drew his eyebrows together, erasing his easy smile. "Seems dangerous out here with unpredictable drivers. You don't know what they're thinking."

Caroline crossed her arms over her chest and cocked her head.

"I know," he said. "Like me." He reached onto the floor of his truck and picked up an orange hard hat. "At least put this on, just in case."

Caroline had already noticed Matt was wearing his safety yellow hard hat with Dunbar written in black marker on the side.

"I never go anywhere without mine," he said. "Grocery shopping, golf course, piano lessons. I tell you, it's a dangerous world."

Caroline did not want to smile. She was supposed to be threatening him with the letter of the law if he didn't get his giant truck out of the way. But he amused her, even if she did wonder what was under the surface of his ready smile.

"You take piano lessons?" she asked.

"No, but if I did, it would be dangerous. Probably need ear protection, too."

Cars behind him started honking. The noise swelled into a chorus. The tollbooth supervisor poked his head out and gave Caroline a questioning look.

"You have to move your truck," Caroline repeated.

"I know. I have work to do."

"Then what are you doing idling here?"

"Just saying hello. I respect your diligence in guarding my project."

"That's my job," Caroline said.

"I know. But you seem really dedicated. And I just wanted you to know how much I appreciate it." He took off his hard hat and ran his fingers through his short blond hair. His usual easy smile disappeared and a worry line creased his forehead. "I have a lot riding on it."

Of course he did. It was a multimillion-dollar venture. But something about his tone made Caroline wonder how deep his personal stakes went.

"If you appreciate my work, you can get moving so I won't get fired," she said.

"I'll make sure you get doughnuts tomorrow. And I'll bring some for your giant bodyguard, too."

Matt smiled. Started his truck. And rolled away with the window still down. He waved a moment later, letting her know he saw her watching him pull away.

"He's not my bodyguard," she said, even though she was the only one within earshot.

She'd known Matt Dunbar for only a week, but already he mystified her. And confounded her. This summer was about two things: getting to the bottom of a mysterious death and getting into the police academy. Wasting her time chatting up construction engineers was not on her agenda.

Last night, she'd visited the records request website for the state department that handled inspection of amusement park rides. It was a long shot, but she'd hoped the records would be online. They weren't. Instead, there was a form to complete with a promise of receiving the records via post in four to six weeks.

Four to six weeks. It was the end of May now, so it would easily be the Fourth of July before anything appeared in the post office box she'd rented in downtown Bayside. Waiting was an eternity, but she planned to fill the time by asking questions.

Caroline took out her frustration on the line of cars backed up on the Point Bridge, directing them into lanes with snappy, uncompromising movements. A man put on his turn signal, trying to move over to a lane he thought was better. Caroline stared him down until he sheepishly turned off the signal and fell into line.

When her tour of traffic duty was over, Caroline hitched a ride in the yellow traffic pickup truck to the front gate. She showed her employee badge at the turnstile on the far right, even though her black Starlight Point Police Department uniform probably made it unnecessary. Rules were rules.

She walked toward the old-fashioned carousel near the front gate. With its hand-painted horses, authentic organ music and brightly lit canopy, it had welcomed guests for decades.

After she passed the carousel, Caroline could see all the way down the midway to the spot where it divided into two paths. One would take guests past roller coasters and a swath of family rides. It also included a gate leading to the long, sandy beach and the historic Lake Breeze Hotel, which had reopened this season with a spectacular renovation. The brainchild of her new sister-in-law, Evie Hamilton, the century-old hotel had retained all its history while being upgraded with modern conveniences.

Instead of following the path to the beachfront hotel, Caroline took the left branch, which led past the construction zone for the new ride. That walkway eventually became the Western Trail, winding under shade trees and by a gristmill, blacksmith's shop and the other historic attractions that made up the Wonderful West. In the far back of the park, both paths met near the Western train station, the Starlight Saloon and a shooting gallery.

Although Caroline enjoyed walking the Western Trail—it was the quietest place in the park—she had only thirty minutes for lunch before she would relieve the police officer by the construction fence. She headed for the station, where a peanut butter sandwich, an apple and an indulgent chocolate cupcake waited for her.

The cable cars overhead cast shadows on the concrete midway. Flowers spilled from planter boxes. The sound of roller coaster trains clacking up hills mixed with the screams of riders going down hills.

She loved it. Loved the smell of funnel cakes and the sound of the waves on the beach. Almost as much as she loved wearing a badge.

Caroline waved to a few friends on her way down the midway. Last summer, she'd met people who worked the food stands and rides, and many of them were back again this year, working their way through college.

Her college days were behind her, though, now that she had satisfied her parents' number one requirement: a bachelor's degree. After achieving that, she was free to do whatever she wanted.

Scott had used his fire science degree to catapult him to leadership on a local fire department and now as the chief at the Starlight Point Fire Department. She planned to use her criminal justice degree to accelerate to the top of the class at the police academy.

A petite blonde girl stepped out from the caricature stand and waved to Caroline. "Come over, we're having a slow day," she said.

Like most of the teenagers who worked at the booth, Agnes was an art student. Her job was to persuade visitors to slow down, have a seat in the shade and wait while their picture was drawn. Caroline had seen the cartoonish drawings many times, such as a woman with a big smile holding a tube of toothpaste and a toothbrush. A man wearing a chef's hat and holding frying pans in both hands. A little girl wearing ballet slippers with musical notes swirling around her head.

Caroline wondered what her caricature would look like. Would she be depicted as a dog sniffing out crimes? A big stern face at the wheel of a police car? She smiled at her friend and said, "I'm on lunch right now."

"Good. Sit down and I'll draw you."

Caroline laughed. "I don't think so."

"Come on, why not? It only takes a minute for me to get the outlines of your face, and then you can come see the finished product later."

Caroline hesitated. She was in uniform. If guests saw a police officer sitting for a portrait, they would either think this was the safest amusement park in the world or the most lackadaisical.

"Maybe later," she said. As she spoke, she noticed a framed caricature on the wall. An example made to entice customers, it was fully colored and remarkably well-done. The man in the picture was wearing a yellow hard hat and driving a dump truck. A big blue and green ball representing the planet Earth was in the bed of the truck.

"That's a really good one," Agnes said, noticing Caroline's stare. "Done by one of my friends this year. I think it's his brother in the picture."

"Is his last name Dunbar?"

Agnes tilted her head and raised her eyebrows. "Yeah, how did you know?"

"I've met him."

"Then maybe you can tell me why he's got the whole world in his truck. I asked Lucas, but he just shrugged and said you had to know the guy."

Interesting. Matt had a younger brother who was an artist. And the artist chose to depict Matt like this.

"I…uh…don't actually know him," Caroline said. "We've just met a few times. Sorry I can't help you. I better grab my lunch before break's over."

"Come back and I'll do your portrait when you're not wearing that ugly uniform," Agnes said. "I'm going to draw you in a red evening gown. With a badge and gun, of course."

When Caroline finished her lunch and

took up guard duty, the hours ticked by. Slowly. There were no heavy machinery noises from the other side of the fence. Probably because it was Saturday, she thought. For all she knew, Matt had stayed for less than an hour and was now home catching up on whatever was on his DVR. She wondered where he lived. Did he have a house in Bayside? Had he lived there all his life?

What did she know about the guy? He was a construction engineer entrusted with a massive project. Jack Hamilton seemed to like him. He had broad shoulders, a smile that lit his eyes and a line around his head from wearing a hard hat.

Caroline shifted from foot to foot. Heat curled the hairs that escaped her long ponytail and stuck to her neck.

She made up sarcastic answers to the summer's number one question, even though she forbade herself to ever use them. *What are they building, you ask?*

A funeral home and crematorium.

A baseball diamond.

A track for camel racing.

She watched the Scrambler flash and swirl across the midway. Counted the number of ice cream cones passing her by. Watched children skip along beside their parents.

And tried to put Matt out of her mind so she could focus on her summer goal: figure out what happened that night on the Loose Cannon back in 1985.

MATT SAT ON the tailgate of his pickup, waiting for his stepfather to stop by the construction site after closing the office for the day. While he swung his legs, taking the weight off his tired feet, he thought about Caroline.

He found her interesting. She guarded his construction zone, an invaluable ally making sure no one got in to vandalize or slow down their work with a moment of misplaced curiosity. He liked having her outside the fence with her look of determination.

But he also wondered why she was so quick with the information about the Loose Cannon and then so evasive when he questioned her. No matter how much she intrigued him, nothing was more important than securing Bruce Corbin's trust by making sure his family never had another failure like the one long buried.

Matt knew his stepfather believed in him.

Bruce hadn't been forced to give Matt the job of construction engineer; there were other choices. But this job was also a test. Could someone with only a few years of on-the-job experience complete such a massive project? Was a master's degree in construction engineering a substitute for age and experience?

Bruce Corbin drove through the open gate and Matt shoved it closed and locked it behind his stepfather's truck.

Looking every one of his sixty-five years, Bruce climbed slowly out of his truck. His face was deeply lined from years of working outdoors. Since his brother John's death over the winter, Bruce seemed to have aged ten more years.

"Looking good, Matt," Bruce said, his voice raspy.

He leaned heavily on his truck, took a deep breath that moved his entire chest and gestured toward the construction area. Mounds of dirt. Holes ten feet deep. Dump trucks. Earthmoving machinery.

It was a mess.

"I love the smell of dirt," Bruce said. "It's the smell of something getting done."

"Most people would think we're not getting much done."

"Most people don't know diddly about building something this big."

Do I know diddly about building something this big?

Matt leaned against the truck next to his stepdad. "It's been slow work digging out concrete footers from the previous construction on the site." He watched his stepfather's face, then added, "Big footers."

"I know what you're talking about," Bruce said. "It was that roller coaster my brother's company built. I knew they were there when I bid this job."

Although he was tempted to ask about the taboo subject, Matt saw the grief in Bruce's expression and didn't press him. Bruce's congestive heart failure took more and more out of him every day, and Matt knew his mother was worried.

"We'll have them all out in a few more days."

"Good."

"So we're still on track with the project," Matt said. "It would help, though, if some of the old blueprints were still around."

Bruce shook his head. He drew another long breath. "Destroyed. All of them. Years ago."

"It's a little ironic," Matt said, his voice quiet. "Digging up something Uncle John built and putting something new in its place."

He was taking a huge risk. The Loose Cannon was a shadowy topic in their family, something he'd realized in subtle ways in the twelve years his mother had been married to Bruce.

The ride was a failure, but it wasn't the construction company's fault. Starlight Point had decided to dismantle the ride after only one season, and his uncle's company got the contract to tear down something they'd just built. It had, according to whispered family stories, broken his uncle's spirit and caused him to sell the company to his brother. A boon for Bruce Corbin, but Matt suspected his uncle had never been the same since. John moved thirty miles away and started a small home renovation company with a few trusted employees.

Matt hoped he wouldn't follow in his uncle's footsteps. He wouldn't let this ride be a failure if he could help it. He wouldn't let down his family, not when there was so much at stake—for Starlight Point and for himself. A success in the location of an old failure might help Bruce let go of his grief for his brother and give him hope for the future.

Bruce cleared his throat but didn't say anything.

Matt was sorry he'd brought it up, sorry for the sorrow on Bruce's face. He needed to change the subject or he was afraid his step-father would cry, and tears from the venerable old man who had changed his life were not something Matt could handle.

"I'm giving this project everything I've got," Matt said. "I'll make you proud."

Bruce laid a huge hand on Matt's shoulder. "I know you will, son."

CHAPTER FOUR

"IS THIS THE best you can do on your day off? Have lunch with your brother?" Scott asked.

Caroline pointed at the windows of the employee cafeteria, which were streaked with heavy raindrops. "You're my rainy day plan. And you usually buy my lunch, unless I'm being particularly difficult and you're mad at me."

"If I spring for an extra pudding parfait, will you consider my alternate career plan for you?"

Caroline rolled her eyes. This was a conversation so old it was practically scripted.

"I'm not going to become a kindergarten teacher."

"Zoologist?"

"No."

"Librarian?" he suggested.

"No."

"Dog walker. And that's my final offer."

Caroline grabbed a handful of fries from her brother's plate and took her time chewing them. "I'm thinking of joining the Marines. I want to work on my upper body strength."

"No pudding parfait for you," Scott said.

Caroline laughed. "I'll go easy on you and be a nice safe cop instead of a marine."

Scott cleared his throat and drew his eyebrows together. Caroline knew the expression well, had labeled it the *big brother* look. *Here it comes.*

"You know Evie and I have an extra room in our apartment downtown. In case you'd like to escape the heat in the employee dorm. You'd have your own shower. Air conditioning. A fridge full of whatever you want."

"And the privilege of living with two newlyweds who are disgustingly in love. One of whom is my boss."

"I'm not really your boss."

"I didn't mean you," Caroline said. "And I like the employee dorms. My friends are there. It's a short walk to work. If there's any serious action going down, I'm right there ready to get in it."

Scott's frown deepened. "Those dorms

are a fire hazard. I'm trying to tolerate them for one more season knowing they're being replaced this fall," he said. "I may burn them down myself in October."

"My brother, Mr. Fire Safety, would burn something down?"

"It would be a good training session for the fire department. Can never get enough training."

Caroline shoved her tray aside and uncapped her bottle of water.

"I probably shouldn't be eating this greasy food. If the rain stops, I'm going to go for a run along the water downtown later."

"Are you worried about passing the running test for the police academy?"

"Not worried about passing. I want to beat all the other guys."

Scott laughed. "You probably will."

Caroline leaned back in her chair and crossed one leg over the other. She watched her brother shovel in his food.

He wore his Starlight Point Fire Department uniform. His name tag said Chief Bennett, a promotion he'd earned through a combination of his education, experience and a heroic rescue of Evie Hamilton from a burning building the previous season. No doubt, her brother was a hero. He'd always been hers.

He worked part-time for the city of Bayside's fire department, acted as the fire inspector for new construction in the city and led the department at Starlight Point. His inspector's job was a major area of conflict between him and Evie when they were working through the hotel renovation plans last summer, but they'd both managed to come out with their dreams intact. And he might be able to help his little sister, too.

"Do you have access to construction plans from a long time ago?" Caroline asked.

Scott glanced up from his plate. "How long?"

"1985."

"That depends on a lot of things. What's in the plans you want to see?"

"A roller coaster. The Loose Cannon that was here for just that one season."

He shrugged. "The museum in the town hall back in the Wonderful West probably has pictures of it. You could start there."

"There aren't any," Caroline said. "I looked."

Scott crossed his arms and gave her the

big brother look. "Is this how you're spending your summer?"

"A girl was killed on that ride. Maybe you could ask Evie what she knows about it."

"The Hamiltons didn't own this place in 1985, and I don't plan to ruin dinner any night this week by bringing up what is probably a sore subject."

Heat crept over her neck and face and her heart hammered. Of all people, she would expect her brother to understand her quest for justice and answers. "The girl who was killed, do you know who she was?"

"Should I?" Scott looked perplexed but interested.

"The Knights who live down the street from Mom and Dad's old house."

"The Silent Knights?"

Caroline rolled her eyes. "Do you know why they were so quiet and reclusive, why they moved to Yorkville years ago? They were trying to get away from here. It was their daughter who was killed. She was only twelve. And they never found out what caused the accident. They never got closure or justice. It's not right."

"How do you know this?"

"They told me a few weeks ago when I was helping Mom and Dad move. I was wearing a Starlight Point sweatshirt while I was hauling stuff to the moving van. I guess they decided to say something before our family moved away for good."

Caroline swirled a fry through a puddle of ketchup. Her jaw was tight and she couldn't look at her brother. "She was only twelve," she whispered.

Scott reached over and squeezed Caroline's hand. "Sometimes you have to let things go and move on. No matter how hard I enforce fire safety codes, it won't bring back our sister. And no matter how doggedly you seek justice for every crime, it won't—"

"Hey, you two." Evie stood at their table holding a dripping umbrella in one hand and two pudding parfaits in her other. She put the parfaits in the center of the table. "You look like you need these. I could see you were bickering clear over there." She cocked her head, indicating the cafeteria line.

"We weren't exactly squabbling," Scott said. He moved over a chair and made room for Evie to sit. As soon as she did, he put an arm around her and kissed her temple.

"Very cute," Caroline said. "And thanks for the dessert."

"Is your brother harassing you about becoming a police officer, living in the fire hazard employee dorms or both?"

Caroline gave Evie a lopsided grin and dug into her dessert without responding. Evie already knew the answer. It was nice that she'd shown up when she did. Caroline and her brother had had this conversation before. They used to be more in tune, both of them using their chosen profession to right an old wrong. But Scott had changed in the past year, letting the tragic death of their older sister, Catherine, go.

Caroline was afraid to let it go, afraid she'd forget the sister she'd never even gotten a chance to know.

DOWNPOURS ON CONSTRUCTION sites were the worst, Matt thought as he gave up and sent his crew home after lunch on a relentlessly rainy Tuesday. He sat in his truck for half an hour, refreshing the radar on his phone over and over, but it was no use. The rain might move off and make a beautiful evening, but the work day was doomed. Judging from the rivers running through the mud, the next few days weren't going to be pretty.

Matt drove through the gate onto the outer loop, turned on his truck's flashers, and ran back in the rain to close and secure the gate. As he snapped the lock together, he saw a familiar figure dashing across the road with an umbrella.

Caroline appeared to be leaving the marina gate and crossing over to the employee dorms. She wasn't wearing her uniform and Matt realized it must be her day off.

He dashed back to his truck and pulled onto the road to head to his office. Caroline didn't really live in those old dorms, did she? Somehow, he'd imagined the sister-in-law of the owners living in the Hamilton compound or in the luxury employee dorms. Which didn't seem to exist, now that he thought about it.

It would be a few hours before he saw his own small house in Bayside. His crew couldn't pour footers and prep the site for the new ride, but he could always find work to do at the construction office.

The Shooting Star/Super Star roller coaster was not the only project Bayside Construction had going on. For the sake of the family business, he needed to prove he could juggle multiple projects without dropping one.

Through his office wall, he heard his stepfather coughing. He ignored it for a few minutes out of habit, something he'd gotten sadly used to over the past year. After hearing body-wracking coughs for almost ten minutes, though, Matt went to the small office kitchen and made a cup of tea with a healthy dose of honey. He walked into Bruce's office and set it quietly on his desk.

"Sounds like you need this," he said.

"It's the damp weather. I'd say it's the damn weather, but your mother doesn't like that."

Bruce inhaled the steam from the tea and gestured for Matt to sit.

"Marrying your mother is the best thing that's ever happened to me."

"Likewise, I think," Matt said. He didn't like his stepfather's gray skin and labored breathing. He watched the older man drink the tea. "Want me to call your doctor for you?"

His stepfather shook his head. "Won't do any good. He's said what he's got to say about it. Truth is, I don't have much time left and there's no sense denying it."

"I hope that's not true," Matt said. He swallowed, his throat thick.

"I might as well tell you, I love you like a son. But my main concern is making sure your mother's provided for. She volunteered at the church and women's shelter all these years, so she has no retirement money coming."

"I'll take care of her."

"I know you want to. And I believe in you. But running this company is hard. Takes a lot out of you."

"It sounds like there's something you want to tell me."

"Haven't decided anything. Seems I've got two options. Sell the company and set your mother up with a nice amount of money to live on. It would pay for Lucas to finish college, too."

Matt held his breath, wondering and fearing what his stepfather's choice would be.

"I appreciate you paying for my college," he said slowly. "Lucas deserves the same."

"My other option is to leave the whole business to you," Bruce said. He put both palms on his desk and looked at Matt expectantly.

Matt didn't know what to say. He wanted the business. Had been training to run it. Believed he had the knowledge and work ethic. But how did he look his stepfather—the man who had practically saved his mother, brother and himself—in the eye and talk about taking over when he died?

A fit of coughing distracted Bruce while Matt sat there feeling helpless and miserable. Would his mother have greater security and comfort from the revenue of the sale of the business or would she be better off if he took it over? What if he failed?

"I would do anything for my family," Matt said. "Our family."

"That's what I was hoping you'd say."

Later in the afternoon, the rain gradually lessened and the skies brightened. Matt was glad to see the clock on the office wall indicate closing time. His stepfather had gone home an hour earlier, so Matt unplugged the coffeepot, turned out the lights, and walked to the parking lot with their secretary and bookkeeper, Nelma.

"Nice evening," Nelma commented.

"It is," Matt agreed. "But what we need is good construction weather. Dry weather."

"Maybe tomorrow," the older lady said as she got in her car.

Matt drove to the brick house he rented. It was larger than a single guy needed, but he liked the style and the price was right. He had a back porch and a yard, an adequate kitchen and a living room where he could watch home improvement shows. He had more shows recorded than he'd ever find time to watch, but he was saving them up for winter, the slow season for construction in Michigan.

Instead of microwaving dinner or parking himself in front of the television, he went upstairs and put on his running clothes. He was often too tired for an evening run after working on-site all day, but he'd spent the afternoon behind a desk. And he had plenty of stress to burn off.

He rode his bike downtown to the waterfront, locked it in a bike rack and started a warmup jog on the asphalt path that wound along the water's edge. Almost three miles long, it provided views of the harbor, the boat docks, a park and the bay. Across the bay, on a peninsula jutting between Bayside and Lake Huron, was Starlight Point. The roller coasters, the giant wheel and the Star Spiral dominated the skyline and provided a light show at night. He often walked, ran or biked on the path, a habit he'd developed in junior high and never outgrew.

He passed the city marina, where his stepfather had a sailboat docked. Bruce hadn't been out on the boat this year, and Matt wondered if he'd be able to this summer. Would he live to see next summer? Each day seemed to take a greater toll. As he jogged along, Matt tried to imagine what it would feel like to be facing the end of his life and trying to leave things sorted for the people he left behind.

He picked up his pace, wishing he could outrun his problems. He'd tried outrunning the fact that his biological father spent his days in a ten-by-ten-foot prison cell, a punishment he richly deserved even though serving the sentence didn't erase what he'd done to his family. What he'd done to his trusting wife and two young sons.

His heart hammered and his breath was short. A stitch tortured his side and one of his shoelaces started flapping. Matt made himself slow down to a walk. Put his hands on his hips and breathed deeply.

"I was going to challenge you to a race," a voice said behind him. "But you were running as if you were trying to dodge a tornado."

Matt turned to see Caroline, hands on her hips, catching her breath. Her long dark hair was in a ponytail and she wore a sleeveless red shirt and black shorts. Her cheeks were pink and her eyes bright. It was the first time he'd talked to her when she was not wearing a black police uniform.

"Never outran a tornado," he said. "But I did see a waterspout on the lake once."

"Here?" Caroline asked, gesturing at the lake.

"Just a little ways down the shore. We were at a family picnic that folded up pretty fast after that."

"So you grew up here in Bayside?"

"I've lived here since I was fourteen." He didn't care to explain the first part of his life in a city a few hours away. "So, are you staying in shape so you can chase the bad guys?"

She laughed. "Of course. I just hope you

don't commit any crimes. I couldn't catch up to you."

"I don't usually run that fast. And I can't do it very long. It was just one of those days."

She smiled and nodded sympathetically. "I have those days."

Matt was afraid he was on the brink of telling her every single one of his problems. He controlled himself and did the sensible thing instead. He knelt and tied his loose shoelace.

"It was my day off," Caroline said. "But it rained."

"Is it better to have a rainy day off than to stand in the rain outside my construction fence?"

She shrugged. "I have a raincoat. And I've made friends with a huge tree that probably attracts lightning but also keeps me dry."

"Want to run together?" Matt tried to use the same tone he might use with a friend or with his brother. Although there was something about Caroline that made him feel cautious, he knew he'd miss her company when he went home tonight.

She twirled her earbuds. "My batteries

are dead, so I'd rather walk. If you're ready for a cooldown," she added.

"Sure."

They fell into step together. It reminded Matt of the first time they met several weeks ago when she marched him back to his tent.

"Do you live in the employee dorms by the marina?"

"I do."

He caught her glaring at him. She stopped and threw up her hands. "Stop it," she said. "That's the same look my brother gives me whenever the subject comes up."

"He doesn't like it?"

"He's the fire chief at the Point and he's sure the dorm is a big matchbox."

Matt was relieved to see a small smile return to her face. She wasn't mad.

"I'd be more worried about it falling down," he said. "Have you ever looked at the roofline? It waves like a flag."

"Maybe they built it that way," she said, resuming her walking pace.

"Right," Matt said. "More likely it's sitting on unstable ground and it's shifted here and there until you could probably shove it over with your car."

Caroline's eyes narrowed in concentration. "Is the ground at Starlight Point unstable?"

An odd question for her to ask. Her expression right now said *investigative cop*.

"It's a peninsula on the lake. Of course there are moisture issues and sand."

"And that contributes to the failure of a building or...other things over time?"

"Tough questions," he said. "You'd be better off asking a soil engineer."

They walked in silence a few minutes until they got to the parking lot at the end of the path. Matt stopped at the bike rack. "Here's my ride," he said.

"Mine's over there." Caroline pointed to an older vehicle that looked like a former police car. It didn't have official decals, but it still had a spotlight attached to the driver door.

"Nice, huh?" she said, smiling. "I bought it at a police auction for five hundred bucks."

He laughed. "You don't drive that on dates, do you?"

"Not yet," she said. She waved and walked across the lot.

"See you tomorrow," Matt yelled.

She acknowledged him with a head bob as she climbed into her silver car. Matt watched her drive away, already looking forward to seeing her the next day at Starlight Point.

CHAPTER FIVE

IF IT HADN'T been so early in the morning and so quiet, Caroline might not have heard the crunch and the swearing. Without the luxury of air conditioning in the employee dorms, she kept her window open night and day. Her window faced the construction zone, and she considered it her responsibility to keep watch even when she wasn't on duty.

She jumped out of bed and went to the window. A dump truck was creeping away from one of the traffic pickups parked outside the construction gate. The traffic truck wasn't usually there. And she could see how the dump truck driver might not have seen the smaller truck as he backed through the gate. It was understandable.

The dump truck driver got out and slammed his door. Caroline watched as he walked back and inspected the front fender of the yellow traffic pickup. He pulled the hem of his work shirt loose and rubbed the paint on the fender. Looked around. Looked over his shoulder.

And got back in his truck as if nothing had happened.

Caroline took in a sharp breath and grabbed the shorts and shirt she'd worn last evening after she got off work. Slid her feet into sneakers without slowing down for socks. She grabbed her phone and raced down the stairs. The truck was making a careful three-point turn and it was obvious what the driver's plan was.

He was fleeing the scene.

She dashed across the road and held up her hand, traffic-cop style, in front of the dump truck. The sun was just up, but she had no doubt the driver could see her. His window was down and he had one thick arm resting on the open frame. He stuck his head out the window.

"Problem, lady?"

"Yes, there is. You backed into that truck," she said, pointing at the yellow pickup without taking her eyes off the driver.

He cocked his head and Caroline could see him thinking about a way out of it.

"Is it your truck?"

What kind of stupid question was that?

"No, it belongs to Starlight Point," she said, trying to keep her voice cool.

"Then it's none of your business."

"It's everyone's business, especially those of us who work here."

"Did you actually see me back into it?"

Rage bubbled up in her throat. She wanted to lie. Desperately. Wanted to say that she had seen it with her own eyes. But it wasn't the truth. Not exactly the truth. And she was an officer of the law. She risked a glance at the damaged truck. The morning sun glinted off the yellow fender's large dent. The bumper was crinkled and the headlight broken.

"I heard it," she said. "And when I looked out my window, I saw you rubbing your truck's paint off the fender. Trying to destroy evidence."

"Maybe I was just cleaning it," he said. "Construction zones are dirty. There wasn't nobody in the truck, and nobody actually saw anything. You should go back to bed and let me do my job."

Caroline put her fisted hands on her hips and shook her head. "You know what you did. I'm Officer Bennett of the Starlight Point Police Department. Step out of the truck."

She had no badge, no gun, no uniform and no radio. All she had was tangled hair, a college T-shirt, good posture and the cop face she'd practiced in her mirror. She had no backup, but she had justice on her side. If she did nothing, some seasonal employee would be blamed for the damage to that traffic truck. Starlight Point's insurance company would be stuck with the bill. She wasn't standing by and letting it go.

The burly dump truck driver sat back in his seat and stared at her through his windshield. *I've got him. He's going to give up without a fight.*

And then he laughed at her. Crossed his arms over his belly and laughed. Caroline stood her ground in the middle of the road, snapped a picture of his license plate with her phone and hit the speed dial number for Starlight Point's police dispatcher. She relayed a quick report of a noninjury accident and gave her location so a uniformed officer could come out and write a report.

The driver stared defiantly while she called it in, and Caroline realized she was in for a long two-minute wait for someone to come over from the station. If she could arrest the driver for mocking her, she'd do it. But she would settle for busting him on leaving the scene of an accident if he tried to drive away before backup arrived.

Her indignation churned into adrenaline when the driver swung open his door and stepped out. He was twice her size and moved toward her with an ugly expression. Even if she called dispatch again and asked for emergency backup, it would still take a few minutes for anyone to arrive. Caroline had self-defense down to a science, but the truck driver had size and anger in his arsenal.

The last thing she wanted to do was back down, but she was almost considering it when she heard a loud truck right behind her on the outer loop road. Given the time of day and location, it was almost certainly a construction vehicle.

Great. Construction workers probably stick together.

The driver turned off the engine. She heard the squeaking of a window being rolled down.

"Is there a problem?" a voice behind her asked.

A familiar voice.

She looked over her shoulder and saw Matt Dunbar at the wheel of a blue pickup, his yellow hard hat in place as always, but his usual smile replaced with a look of worry. His eyes met hers for a moment as if he was assessing her.

The driver had stopped his advance, but his menacing expression and tense body language remained obvious and reminded Caroline how lucky she was Matt had come along at the right moment.

"There is a problem," she said clearly, her words reverberating off the fence in the silent morning air. "One of your trucks backed into that parked vehicle. And the driver is trying to deny it."

Matt's attention swung from the pickup to Caroline and his look of concern deepened. "Anybody hurt?"

"Not yet. Just property damage," Caroline said. She liked that his first question was about potential injuries. It was a definite mark in his favor. Arriving just in time to save her from a fight was also a giant red check in the plus column.

"Good," he said. "Let me pull off the road and we'll do the paperwork."

"Didn't you hear what I said? Your driver is denying it."

Matt laughed, his tense expression replaced by something closer to his usual smile. "That man behind you is not my driver, but he is delivering stone for my project so I feel responsible for his actions. If he worked for me, I'd fire him."

"For an accident?"

Matt shoved his hard hat back on his forehead. "I'd fire him for trying to lie his way out of it. And whatever else he was about to do. That's not how I operate."

"Come on," the dump truck driver said. "That damage could have been there already. I can't stick around all day and fill out reports. I'm supposed to be back at the quarry for another load of stone right now."

Although it was technically her jurisdiction and she was the one standing in the middle of the road stopping traffic, Caroline waited, curious about how Matt would handle the situation.

He took off his seat belt. Got out of his truck. Stalked over so he was nose-to-nose with the driver. "You will pull off the road. You will cooperate with this police officer. Or your company will never do business with mine again."

The hard steel in Matt's voice made Caroline glad she wasn't in the other man's shoes.

"You don't really think that girl's a cop, do you?" the burly driver asked.

And that's the end of my sympathy for that guy.

Caroline dialed on her phone and gave the dispatcher an update as she watched Matt reach in and take the keys out of the dump truck's ignition.

MATT INSPECTED THE back of the dump truck. A minor dent and some yellow paint would probably not be noticed by the truck's owner. But the yellow Starlight Point traffic pickup was not so lucky. It needed serious attention to its front corner, bumper and headlight.

Despite the relatively small section of damage, Matt knew the cost could run into the thousands. When his mother had backed into his stepfather's car in the driveway last year, it was a similar toll.

A Starlight Point police cruiser pulled up and the chief got out. Matt waited while Caroline approached her boss and gave him a quick explanation. His day would be going a lot more smoothly right now if he were inside the gate supervising his crew as they used the stone to pack the newly poured footers for the ride. But there was no way he was going to make an enemy of anyone at Starlight Point—especially Caroline—by glossing over a serious infraction.

She was gesturing with her hands as she talked with her boss. No doubt she'd already exchanged words with the dump truck driver before he'd pulled up. What would have happened if Matt hadn't shown up when he did? Would the other guy have continued to give Caroline a hard time? Left the scene of the accident? Or worse?

Matt had an odd sensation in his chest when he thought of Caroline facing down big burly jerks like the guy driving the dump truck. Smart and tenacious, she could take care of herself as well as anyone. But life wasn't always fair. He'd learned that the hard way watching his father make the mistake of flouting the law.

He would never forget the day his biological father was led off in handcuffs, despite his assurances it would never happen.

Caroline usually wore her long brown hair in a tight ponytail, but her clothing and the time of day made it clear she'd just gotten out of bed. Matt pictured her flying from her bunk in the dorms to stomp out injustice. He smiled just imagining it.

Caroline glanced in his direction and he felt as if a searchlight had caught him making a prison break. He hoped she wouldn't ask him why he was staring at her and grinning. What if she thought he was mocking her or not taking the accident seriously?

He sobered his expression. She was waving him over to talk with her and her boss. Matt crossed the road, the keys from the dump truck jingling in his shirt pocket.

"Dunbar," the chief said. "Heard you happened along at the right time."

Matt wondered what Caroline had told her boss about the driver's apparent refusal to cooperate. He didn't want to imply Caroline couldn't have handled it herself.

"Or the wrong one," Matt said, shaking the chief's hand. "If I'd been here a little earlier, I might have prevented the dump truck from backing into your pickup. Wish I had."

"That would have ruined Caroline's fun. She hasn't gotten to arrest anyone this season."

Caroline narrowed her eyes at her boss. "Hey, it's only June. Give me time."

"If it's okay with you," Matt said, addressing Caroline, "I'd like to get that truck off the road. Can I pull it inside the construction fence while you write up the charming driver? It seems like a hazard on this narrow road."

"Fine by me," she said.

Matt started the engine while the dump truck driver leaned sullenly against the fence. The police chief inspected the yellow traffic truck while Matt drove through the gate. He stepped down from the driver's seat and found Caroline waiting by his door.

"Thanks," she said. "For what you did."

"I didn't do much," he replied. "Just encouraged him to own up to his mistake."

Matt held out the keys to the dump truck but Caroline shook her head.

"We'll release him in a few minutes after we get a copy of his license and write him a ticket. He can make his trip to the quarry for more stone."

"I'm sure he'll appreciate that. But he might want to trade jobs with someone and send a different truck back here," Matt said.

"Do you have a lot more stone trucks coming in?"

Matt nodded. "Shoring up the footers for the top secret ride you probably don't know anything about."

Caroline smiled. "I heard they were building an office supply store here."

"A thrilling one."

Caroline glanced over at her boss who was writing on a clipboard while the truck driver stood there, arms crossed over his chest.

"So you already poured the concrete footers," she said. "Are you on track with the project?"

"Almost," Matt admitted. "There are always surprises."

"Like remains from a previous construction on this site?"

Matt took a deep breath. Why was she

asking him about that? "I'd rather not think about the past when I'm trying to make darn sure the future ride is a success."

Caroline's expression reminded him of cop shows on television where someone was getting interrogated in the police tank.

"You've seen the…uh…evidence of the old ride, the Loose Cannon," she continued. "Was there anything that would explain the accident back in 1985?"

Did Caroline know that the company that had built the ride belonged to his stepfather's brother? Was that why she was asking him these questions? If she didn't know already, it wouldn't take her very long to discover the connection. For the sake of honesty and keeping his relationship with her friendly, he should probably just tell her right now.

But he couldn't. The story of that ride had been forbidden in his family for so long it felt strange to talk about it, especially with someone he hardly knew. Someone who seemed to have a dogged sense of justice and a love of investigation.

Might she turn up something he didn't want to know? Not that he believed his family was covering something up, but the failure and subsequent sale of the company made him wonder. He didn't want it dredged up, especially with his stepfather's poor health.

"That was before I was born," Matt said. "I'm afraid you're asking the wrong guy."

Caroline blew out a breath. "I keep trying to find the right person to ask, but—"

The police chief walked up and started taking pictures of the back bumper of the dump truck.

"We'll have him out of here in a few minutes," the chief said, "and then the insurance companies can fight about it."

Matt handed the chief the keys to the dump truck, nodded at Caroline and walked to the open gate to wave in another truck full of stone that had just arrived. Dwelling on an old story wasn't going to help him meet his deadlines, and Caroline's questions made him wonder if he should try to keep his distance from her or keep her close by.

CHAPTER SIX

STARLIGHT POINT TOOK its role as the flagship business of the local community seriously, Matt thought as he ran through the park in the early morning hours. Already this summer, he had endured the Campout for Charity, purchased advance tickets for the Beer and Barbeque for Bikes event on the July Fourth weekend, and today he was running with his brother in the Starlight for Shelters 5K, a race benefiting the local homeless shelter.

The running part was easy. Turning off his brain was the challenge. Everywhere he went, Matt Dunbar saw structures that ignited his engineering imagination. The roof of the Starlight Saloon's porch that probably didn't slope enough for rain runoff. The authentic copper rain gutters on the train station's passenger depot. The emergency staircase spiraling down from the ride platform on a roller coaster.

Although he was no architect, he appreciated the thought and science behind every construction decision. Loved the smell of blueprints and the feel of the paper rolled out under his fingers—even though laptops were replacing paper blueprints on construction sites.

Matt remembered the home he'd grown up in. The wide sandstone steps where his mother had taken his picture on the first day of kindergarten. He should go back there sometime, just to see the Craftsman-style house with an engineer's eye. An adult's eye.

When his mother had remarried, he and his brother had a much larger and finer home. His stepfather's construction company had built it, and Matt and his brother, Lucas, had reveled in having their own rooms joined by a walk-through closet and bathroom. It was a nicer home in every way, but someday nostalgia might take him back to the place where he'd taken his first steps.

Someday. Maybe running with his brother was making him nostalgic.

"Walk break," Lucas said, holding his side and slowing down.

Matt instantly adjusted his pace to match his younger brother's. Their first mile had been strong and they almost kept up with the lead pack, but they had gradually slowed somewhere around the Wonderful West railroad station.

The early morning run had drawn a sizable crowd. Possibly because the entrance price for the race also included a ticket to Starlight Point for the whole day. And a very cool neon orange T-shirt with a roller coaster motif.

"Sorry," Matt said. "I've been running a lot in the past year, but you've probably been too busy at college to run."

"Busy," Lucas said. "Out. Of. Shape." He took breaths between each word and wiped his forehead with the edge of his race T-shirt. "Sorry to…slow you…down."

"Heck, I don't care," Matt said, putting a hand on his brother's shoulder. "I'm here because it's a good cause. They'll get my donation whether I win or not."

They walked along the Western Trail, shade trees blocking the morning sun. Some runners passed them, but there were other walkers around them. The race had started three hours before the park opened, and even the slowest runners would be off the course before the day's crowds arrived.

"Thanks for paying my entrance fee," Lucas said. "I'm thinking of volunteering at the shelter in Bayside. Maybe they need some art on their walls."

"That would be nice. Maybe you could do a mural."

"That's what I was thinking," Lucas said. "I remember the white walls in that shelter where we ended up when the police locked our house and seized everything."

Matt's chest constricted and he risked a look at his younger brother. The brother he'd always tried to protect. "You were only five," he said. Matt had been eleven—too old to be protected from the truth but too young to understand it. "Long time ago. And things have improved considerably for us since then."

"No thanks to dear old Dad," Lucas said. "If he was going to steal all that money, I wish he would've put some away to pay my tuition."

"You can't go to college on embezzled money. Besides, Bruce is covering your tuition. Just like he did mine."

"Two years to go," Lucas said. He cleared his throat and kept his eyes on the trail ahead of him. "I'm sure you're worried about Bruce, too."

Matt thought about the doctor's prognosis that had Bruce making plans for the company's future. His stepfather obviously believed his time was short, but Matt hoped the doctor was wrong, overly solicitous.

"It was a hard winter for him," Matt said. "When Uncle John died, it seemed as if… I don't know." He almost said it seemed as if his stepfather had lost the will to live, but Matt didn't want to think that. Not with the well-being of his mother, his brother and Bayside Construction on the line. Bruce was not a selfish man. He wouldn't want to leave the people he cared about.

Unless he knew they were provided for.

"If things go bad with him," Lucas asked, "what do you think will happen to the family business?"

"We talked about it, Bruce and I," Matt admitted. "He's worried about the future.

Wants to make sure you get to finish school and Mom is set."

"How'd we get so lucky to end up with a stepdad like him?"

"Believe me, I've wondered the same thing," Matt said. "But we've earned his love. And his trust."

"Does that trust include letting you take over the business?"

Matt did not want to talk about this. Not now when so much was on the line. But his brother deserved to know. They'd never held secrets from each other, each of them somehow knowing that their father's legacy of lies ended the day he was sentenced to jail and permanently out of their lives.

"Bruce believes he has two options. Sell the business soon and invest the money for our family. Or take a chance on leaving it to me."

Lucas sucked in a breath. "That's a lot of pressure. But if I were him, I'd take a chance on you."

Matt's throat was tight. The stress of building a major project combined with wondering what the future would bring made his shoulders feel like ropes holding a wild horse. And hearing his brother's confidence in him only made the stakes seem higher.

"I think he'd be taking a chance on us. The company will be yours, too, when you're ready."

Neither of them said anything for a few minutes, and their breath returned to an easy rhythm.

"I could run again," Lucas offered.

They jogged past the midway train station, the Sea Devil and along the fence at the construction zone. The five-kilometer course had started in the parking lot, wound all the way down the Starlight Point peninsula and back, and would end under a balloon arch near the marina. Bagels, bananas and a live band awaited them at the finish, but there were water stations staffed by off-duty employees along the way.

With only a half mile to go as they ran past the scrambler ride, Matt wouldn't usually have stopped at a water station. He didn't need a drink, but he couldn't resist taking a cup from Caroline Bennett's outstretched hand.

He'd spent just enough time with her that

he couldn't run right by. Didn't want to race past without at least saying hello.

A Starlight Point photographer snapped a picture of Matt and Lucas as they slowed down. With their matching T-shirts and similar height and features, even a casual observer would probably peg them for brothers. But Matt had a few more wrinkles and pounds of muscle than his brother, in addition to the six years between them and the major differences between their chosen careers.

Matt had wanted to follow in Bruce Corbin's footsteps ever since his mom remarried. Maybe it was because he'd desperately needed a male role model he believed in. But it was more than that. He loved the smells, sounds and feel of construction work. Liked to feel the dirt under his nails and under the soles of his work boots.

He and his brother had spent some time in therapy with their mother after their father's incarceration. Matt had learned to work out his feelings. Lucas turned to art.

And he was good. His artist's renderings of the new ride were detailed, impressive, and under lock and key at Bayside Construction. They were the drawings submitted to the

Hamiltons for approval and would be shown to the press when the Hamilton family was ready for the grand reveal. It was Matt's dream to have his brother by his side as he took over their stepfather's construction business.

But the future was a work in progress. All he could do at the moment was put one foot in front of the other.

At the water station, Caroline wore shorts and an orange T-shirt similar to the ones handed out to the racers, but hers said Volunteer on the front. Her smile was friendly, but her eyes darted back and forth between him and his brother. Matt knew she would make the connection in seconds. He was actually surprised she hadn't already figured out he had a brother working the art stand.

"So this is the man," she said, pointing to Lucas, "who drew his brother driving a truck with the whole world in the bed."

He had underestimated her, and it was a good reminder not to do that again. Even though she was off duty today, she could see right through him. Did she like what she saw?

"I should have drawn him winning this

race," Lucas said. "If it weren't for me slowing him down, he'd be done by now."

"I'm afraid to run with him," Caroline said affably as she watched both brothers down their small cup of water. "I tried to catch up with him downtown one day and had to give up. I'd have to fake an injury if I were racing him."

"You wouldn't do that," Matt said. Caroline didn't seem like the kind of person who faked anything.

She smiled and cocked her head. "Probably not. But I'll warn you, I'm not a gracious loser."

"I'll remember that."

The midway was littered with paper cups, but Matt tossed his and his brother's in a nearby trash can.

Caroline put a hand lightly on his arm when he jogged back. "Thank you. Most people just throw their cups on the ground."

"I'm not most people," Matt said.

Her eyes widened just a little and she gave a slight nod. "I've noticed."

"Thanks for the drink," Matt said. He turned to his brother. "Strong finish?"

"Right behind you," Lucas said.

CAROLINE'S MORNING AT the water station had gone quickly and would be over in less than an hour. She wondered if she'd been assigned to work with Virginia Hamilton because of her family connection. Whatever the reason, Caroline admired the older lady's energy and spirit.

A few minutes after the Dunbar brothers ran off toward the finish line, the number of racers dwindled to a few packs of walkers and slower joggers.

"I considered walking in the race, but it isn't as much fun now that Betty died," Virginia said.

Caroline swallowed. Who was Betty? Ever since her brother married Evie Hamilton in May, Caroline had felt like a member of the family. But she hadn't met anyone named Betty.

"Did Betty enjoy walking?" she asked, hoping Virginia's answer would provide the clue she needed.

"Used to. But when she got too old, she loved being pulled in a little red wagon I still had from when the kids were young."

The dog. Caroline remembered seeing Virginia pulling a dog in the wagon last summer but she hadn't known its name. At the time, as she'd patrolled the park and noticed the Hamiltons coming and going all over Starlight Point, she would never have imagined that her brother would marry into the family.

Evie had been good for Scott. She challenged him and made him open his heart—no easy task for someone who'd endured such a tragedy in his youth and took himself all too seriously as a result.

Do I take myself too seriously for the same reason?

Caroline grabbed a trash bag and began picking up discarded paper cups.

"Sorry to hear she passed away," Caroline said. "She must have been part of your family for a long time."

"She was fourteen. I'm thinking of getting a puppy this fall while there's still good weather to train her before winter hits."

"My brother always thinks I should get a dog for protection, but he forgets I lived in dorms for three years while I got my degree. You can't have a pet in college dorms."

"And now?"

"Now I'm going to the police academy in Bayside this fall. I hope."

"Will you live with your brother and my daughter?" Virginia asked.

"Maybe. I'll stay in the dorms here until the season ends and then figure it out."

Virginia put an arm around Caroline's shoulders, forcing her to stop picking up trash for a moment. "There's a spare room at my house over on the Old Road if you ever need it. I'd love the company, and I consider you a member of the family."

Caroline's heart expanded in her chest. Virginia was offering her a home? Which was one more reason Caroline should reconsider looking into an old accident that could probably bring bad publicity to the Hamilton family and Starlight Point.

"Thanks," Caroline said. "I'll think about it. And I could help you train a puppy if you get one. I'd certainly rather live with you than newlyweds."

Virginia laughed and filled paper cups for a group of walkers. She handed a cup to an older man Caroline recognized as one of the clerks who worked in cash control near the front gate.

"Why aren't you racing?" the man asked Virginia. "I'm at least twenty years older than you are and I'm out here." He smiled and tipped back his cup of water.

"Next year," Virginia said. "We had such a great turnout for our first time that I think I can look forward to this every June."

The older man crushed his cup and dropped it into the trash can. Like Matt had a few minutes earlier.

It was a small gesture, but something about Matt made her notice all the things he did. He took doughnuts to his crew and made truck drivers take responsibility for their accidents. And he remembered she liked maple frosting.

"That guy was here back when I started," Virginia said after the older man had continued along the course.

"Did you work here?"

Virginia nodded. "Sure did. Summer employee just like everyone else."

Caroline tried to add up the years in her head. It had to be before Virginia married and had kids…and Virginia's oldest son, Jack, was probably almost thirty. Would Virginia have worked at the Point during the summer of 1985?

"That's why Ford and I always insisted our kids had regular summer jobs, doing everything from emptying dumpsters to scooping ice cream to dancing in the shows. Made them appreciate how hard everyone works to make this place what it is."

"Did you scoop ice cream or dance?"

"No." Virginia smiled and shook her head. She looked up at the cable cars that were staged in the station, waiting for the park to open. "I was in rides. The carousel, kiddie rides, the Scrambler, roller coasters. Wherever they put me. There weren't as many rides back then, but it was still fun."

Was it possible Virginia had worked on the Loose Cannon?

"We had the worst uniforms," Virginia said. "It was the eighties, so you wouldn't have thought they'd be all polyester. But they were. I remember a lot of things about that summer, but being hot and itchy is almost at the top of the list." Virginia's smile faded and she looked down at the midway for a moment. "Almost."

This is killing me, Caroline thought. *When in the eighties?*

"Which coasters did you work on?"

"Silver Streak, mostly," Virginia said.

Caroline's shoulders fell. *Darn.*

"But we rotated around a lot and made friends with all the other kids sweating it out in polyester jumpsuits. Some of the rides got a lot more attention and riders, so we gave them breaks sometimes," Virginia continued.

"What was the popular ride that year?" Caroline asked, hoping she sounded like an interested employee of Starlight Point and not a detective nosing around a murder scene.

"You've probably never heard of it. It was short-lived. A roller coaster called the Loose Cannon."

Caroline swallowed. She didn't have to ask what year Virginia had worked there now. This was an incredible break. Virginia Hamilton had been a ride operator the summer of 1985! She had friends who worked the Loose Cannon. Maybe even worked it herself a few times. *How much did she know?*

More important, how much did Caroline dare to ask?

"I've heard of that ride," Caroline said. "Some kind of accident?"

Virginia's affable smile faded. "It was terrible what happened. Two people gone, just like that."

"Two?" Caroline felt as if she were in the middle of city traffic with cars whooshing past her.

The older woman's jaw tightened. "It was a long time ago."

"I knew one girl died on the ride, but there were two?"

Virginia crossed her arms over her chest. Caroline was afraid she'd just crossed a major line, but she was desperate to find out what Virginia meant.

"I think we can close up our water station now," Virginia said. "Race is about over."

Reluctantly, Caroline flipped over their folding table and snapped the legs into their holders. She stacked it next to their chairs for the maintenance truck to pick up and then grabbed an extra trash bag to clean up the midway around their station.

"There's something I'd like to ask you,"

Virginia said. "It's something we've tried to keep in the family, but we needed outside help last year."

Caroline jammed cups into her trash bag, almost afraid to ask what family-type favor Virginia had in mind. Was she going to be let in on the family secrets and then sworn to silence?

"Your brother was kind enough to run my STRIPE program last year. He taught all those fire safety classes to our seasonal and full-time employees."

"I remember," Caroline said. "He made me demonstrate the correct use of a fire extinguisher in front of two hundred people." And she'd had to listen to her coworkers grumble about being forced into Virginia's classes every summer.

Because she thought employees should learn valuable life skills during their time at Starlight Point, Virginia mandated something special every year. Caroline had heard the stories about ballroom dancing lessons, conversational French, cake decorating and basic auto mechanics. Last year was fire safety, and Caroline had no idea what Virginia had planned for this summer.

"The STRIPE program is such a beloved part of the employee experience here," Virginia said.

Caroline kept her head down, searching out stray cups on the midway. *Beloved* was not the word she'd heard for the program in the employee break room and dorms.

"It's a dangerous world out there," Virginia said. "So I thought a perfect topic for this year would be self-defense."

Caroline stood straight and risked eye contact with Virginia. That was actually a good idea.

"And who better to teach it than you?" Virginia asked.

"You want me to teach self-defense?"

The older lady nodded vigorously. "I'll recruit some volunteers to help you, of course, but I think you are the perfect person to teach people how to take down attackers and save themselves if they ever get in a bind. You are one tough cookie."

Caroline smiled. "I want to be a cop so I can help other people, but teaching them to try to save themselves is a very good start."

CHAPTER SEVEN

"AREN'T YOU GLAD it's your day off so you could come along?" Scott asked.

Caroline hated to admit it, but her brother was right. She was having a nice time, and even Scott looked relaxed. Instead of his usual fire department uniform, Scott Bennett wore a light blue button-down and tie. She didn't have to look closely to know the firefighter symbol, a Maltese cross with axes and hoses, was the motif decorating the tie.

"And you look nice," Scott continued. "People probably won't recognize you since you're not wearing your uniform."

"When I got the invitation for the party cruise, I thought I was being asked to provide security. I almost wore my badge and uniform, but Evie texted me and set me straight. She's probably the one who insisted I get an invite anyway."

"Very funny," Scott said. "Don't you know by now that I'm always looking out for you? Besides, the food looks great and this means I don't have to buy your lunch like I usually do."

Scott and Caroline leaned on the outside rail of the Maritime II party boat. A one-hundred-foot-long, double-decker vessel, the boat was known locally for its party cruises on weekends. It was also a popular choice for wedding receptions, graduation parties, birthdays and anniversaries.

"I was surprised by the sudden announcement of a media event," Caroline said. "I've been faithfully keeping the secret about what's behind the construction fence for a month now because the big reveal was supposed to be in August. It's only halfway through June, so what happened?"

Scott sipped his drink and leaned closer to his sister. "Fear of being upstaged. There hasn't been a new ride in three years, and the roller coaster fan clubs and magazines have gone crazy with speculation. Evie told me some of the rumors they've heard."

Caroline shrugged. "Aren't there always

rumors? And I thought it was good to build excitement and speculation."

"Yes, but some of the rumors were getting close enough to the truth to make the Hamiltons uncomfortable. So, today's press cruise is the magic answer. A preemptive strike."

After searching online the previous evening for information regarding the second death on the Loose Cannon, Caroline had thought a lot about Starlight Point's control of media and rumor. It took her a long time to discover there had been two deaths on the date of the Loose Cannon accident, but one of them was unrelated to the ride failure. A maintenance man had died on that same date from an accident. In Virginia's mind, the two deaths were linked. And Caroline had every intention of finding out why.

From her position along the rail on the starboard side of the ship, Caroline had an unobstructed view of Starlight Point. Tall roller coasters, a giant wheel, the Star Spiral and stoic cottonwood trees defined the skyline. As the Maritime II cruised by, Caroline saw the old-fashioned steam train chugging around the perimeter of the park, white smoke rising gracefully with its movement.

"I guess it's a good idea," she said. "Stay in control of the rumors. The press is going to love this event. You might even get your mug in the paper."

"I'll leave that to Evie, June and Jack. I'm just the fire chief who happens to be very lucky in love."

Caroline rolled her eyes. "See why I don't want to live with you?"

Scott laughed. "We should get some food before the reporters gobble it up. The Hamiltons aren't revealing anything until at least halfway through the cruise, and those reporters look hungry."

The members of the press weren't the only guests Caroline had noticed. When she'd accepted the invitation to the afternoon cruise, she'd known for certain Matt Dunbar would be a guest of honor. She wondered if he would wear his yellow hard hat, or at least have its band imprinted on his short blond hair as he usually did.

She'd put thought into her outfit for the day, too. She couldn't wear a uniform, and her supply of dress clothing was limited. After work the night before, she and Agnes had made a trip to the boutique in the Lake

Breeze Hotel. She'd noticed a green dress in the hotel's shop. Having walked by it several times in the past, she'd wondered how it might look on her—just in case she needed a dress. Like now.

Bringing Agnes along for a second opinion, Caroline had tried the dress on and Agnes—with her artist's expertise—had declared it a definite winner. It was sleeveless, knee length and no-nonsense. Except for the wide ribbon sash at the waist. The leaf-green linen contrasted nicely with her tan and her long brown hair, and brought out her green eyes. According to Agnes.

Caroline had looked in the boutique's mirror and seen a cop trying to look like a girl, but she took her friend's advice anyway. She had to wear *something* to the fancy afternoon cruise. And she happened to have tan-colored sandals to wear with it.

Evie walked up with her cell phone in hand. "Smile," she said.

Scott draped an arm around his sister and Evie took the picture. "I'm sending that to your mother," she said. "To prove that you two aren't always in uniform."

"She'll be shocked to see me in a dress," Caroline said.

"I love that dress. I've walked by it in the hotel store five times, but I was never sure I could pull off the color. It's perfect on you, and you look gorgeous," Evie said. "There may be an attractive single reporter on this boat. Want me to find one for you?"

"No," Caroline said. "And that better not be why you invited me."

"I invited you because you're my sister now. And because you're our chief guard at the construction site. And, most of all, because I heard my mother roped you into being the STRIPE sergeant this year and you deserve any and all perks. Consider this a bribe."

Caroline laughed. "Your mother seems determined about her program and taking care of her summer employees. Maybe that's because she used to be a summer hire herself."

Caroline hoped Evie would start talking about her mother's job as a ride operator three decades ago. Did Evie know more about the Loose Cannon? How much did all the Hamiltons know...and how much should she pry? Especially considering she was at this event because they considered her a family member. It was one of the many ways they were nice to her—and everyone.

"My mother has all kinds of determination," Evie said. She tapped on her phone for a moment. "Sent. Your mother will love it."

As Caroline watched her sister-in-law walk away, she noticed a tall blond man in a white shirt and striped tie. His sleeves were rolled to the elbow, showing off muscular forearms.

No hard hat today. Matt stood with Jack Hamilton and a much older man Caroline had seen on the construction site a few times. Matt was describing something, using his hands to paint an imaginary diagram in the air. He was passionate about his work, something she'd admired about him from their first meeting. This should be a big day for him. Was he nervous? Excited?

Matt saw her at the same moment she noticed him. He stopped drawing blueprints in the air and said something to his companions before heading her way.

"I think I'll refill my drink," Scott said. "Unless you need a babysitter."

"If anyone bothers me, I'll flip him over the rail into the lake," Caroline said. "Take your time."

She laid a hand on the steel railing and looked out over the calm blue waters of Lake Huron. The boat had passed the farthest point of the peninsula, so her view was, technically, the water park and beach of Starlight Point.

Matt appeared in her peripheral vision, sparking a little shimmer of anticipation. He'd wasted no time approaching her as soon as he found her in the crowd. What did that mean? There was only one way to find out. She turned and greeted him, speaking before he could say anything.

"This is quite a day for you," she said, smiling.

He swallowed. Rubbed his hands together. "It is."

She nodded toward his empty hands. "You should have some food. At least get a drink."

"Can't."

"Because you're on the job?"

"Because I'm too nervous," he admitted. He dipped his chin and raised his eyebrows.

Caroline thought it oddly endearing that

such a large, confident man could appear so vulnerable.

"Wait a minute," she said. "Aren't you usually Mr. Cheerful, talking your way out of trespassing tickets, holding up traffic on the bridge and making careless truck drivers play nice?"

"It's all a cover," Matt said, leaning close and speaking quietly. "Inside, I'm a wreck. And there's no way I'm hitting the buffet line. Not only do I have to speak in front of all these people and assure them I'll get this giant project done well and on time, but I have to do it in a white shirt. And a tie. And it's hot."

Caroline laughed. He seemed as uncomfortable playing dress-up as she did. He certainly looked good in his crisp shirt, all clean-shaven and smelling like man-soap. Caroline was suddenly very aware of his physical presence. His square jaw, green eyes and blond eyebrows only inches from her invited her to reach out and adjust his collar.

"I'm serious," he continued. "The pressure is killing me."

"Maybe there will be food left after your

presentation. You could live dangerously then."

"There won't be time. As soon as this boat docks, I'm headed to the site. We've got steel beams being delivered, and I want to be there."

"You'd rather be there than here?" Caroline asked.

"I have to be there." He turned and put a hand on the railing right behind her. His arm grazed her back. "And here. But there are some nice things about being here."

Caroline swallowed.

"It's nice to see the chief of my personal security detail," he said, smiling.

Caroline remembered her promise to her brother that she'd flip anyone who bothered her over the rail. And Matt was definitely bothering her. Solidly in her space and causing uncomfortable heat to rise up her neck. But she didn't want to throw him over the rail. She wasn't quite sure what she wanted to do with him.

"And you look—" he began.

"Mr. Dunbar."

Caroline and Matt both glanced up sharply and saw a man with a press badge and a notebook. He was easily sixty years old, and deep wrinkles around his eyes gave him the appearance of someone who was always squinting.

He was a reporter, Caroline thought, always snooping out a story. Maybe she wasn't much different with her quiet digging into an almost-forgotten mystery. He looked familiar and she recalled throwing someone who looked just like him off the property a week ago when he was nosing around asking questions.

"I'd like to talk to you for a piece I'm doing for the *Bayside Times*. I left messages for you at your company and even tried coming out to your site once, but I got turned away by a cop."

The reporter didn't give Caroline any side-eye, so she assumed he didn't recognize her. It had to be the green dress and sandals.

"That's why I'm here today," Matt said, "to talk with the press."

Matt sounded professional but not particularly encouraging. *He probably wishes he was behind the wheel of a construction ve-*

hicle instead of chatting with reporters on a perfectly nice day for building.

"I'll get right to it then. I'm doing a story about the irony of the situation. It must be really strange for you to be building the new ride—that I hope we're going to hear all about today—over the site of the old ride your family built and then had to tear down."

Matt's shoulders stiffened. His jaw tightened. The friendly, almost vulnerable expression Caroline had grown used to was replaced by an entirely different one.

"That was a different company," Matt said, ice in his voice.

"Right. John Corbin owned it. And he sold it to his brother. Your dad."

"Stepdad," Matt said.

The reporter shrugged. "Same difference. So, give me the scoop. Is this a shot at redemption for the family? Your chance to succeed where you previously failed?"

Caroline held her breath, afraid to even blink. This conversation was the last thing she'd expected to hear today, and her brain was turning over the new information rapidly. If the failed Loose Cannon was built by Matt's family, he had to know more than he was letting on. How much did he know, and how much was he trying to cover up?

Matt looked down as if he didn't want her to see what was behind his eyes. Had he been intentionally withholding information from her? So much for finding him conscientious, thoughtful, even attractive. Just like a lot of other people, he clearly had something to hide. And it could be huge.

It was one more reminder to keep her focus where it belonged and not let down her guard.

"Hey," Lucas Dunbar said, appearing out of nowhere and sliding in next to his brother. "Jack Hamilton wants to talk to you if you've got a minute."

"I've got a minute," Matt said. He gave the reporter a hard stare and turned to Caroline.

His expression softened just a little, but she saw something in his eyes she didn't understand. Pain? Regret?

"Talk to you later, Caroline," he said.

He turned and left with his brother, leaving Caroline alone with the reporter. An older reporter who almost certainly knew more about the Loose Cannon incident than she did.

"So," she said. "John Corbin sold his company to his brother."

"Bruce."

She nodded. "Bruce Corbin. Who renamed it Bayside Construction."

"Uh-huh. He's right over there." The reporter pointed to an older man.

In the scant information Caroline had found about the ride, she'd noted the name of the construction company, JC Construction. The initials made sense now. But she had plenty of questions anyway.

"When did that transfer take place?"

"Sometime during the fall of 1985. Not long after the ride came down at the end of the year."

So JC Construction tore down a ride it had built. And then the company officially changed hands and got a new name. There had to be more to that story.

Caroline tried to assume an expression that did not say *investigative reporter* so the journalist wouldn't see her as competition and clam up. She was glad to be wearing a party dress instead of her black uniform.

"Do you know what caused the accident

or anything about the man who died later that night?" she asked.

"Everybody knows about it," the reporter said. "But nobody knows quite what happened. It got ruled an accident. Seems to have been an open-and-shut case."

"A case with strange timing," Caroline said.

The reporter raised an eyebrow and she suspected he recognized her as the Starlight Point police officer who'd walked him to his car in the marina parking lot last week.

"You seem pretty curious about it," he said.

She shrugged. "Everyone loves a mystery. It can't be a coincidence that one of the very few on-the-job fatalities at Starlight Point happened on the same night a coaster failed and a girl was killed."

"Not saying it's a coincidence," the reporter said. "I asked a lot of questions at the time, but nobody had anything to say. And most of those people are dead now, including the guy who built the ride."

The reporter looked beyond Caroline's shoulder and his expression soured. He turned and walked toward a group of men lingering over the food table. When Caroline shifted just enough to glance behind her, her senses alert, she found Bruce Corbin leaning on the railing. He mopped his forehead with a handkerchief, gave her a hard stare and moved off toward his stepsons.

Caroline faced the water and the view of the Lake Breeze Hotel. In only a few minutes, the boat would turn and head back to the bay where the big revelation of the new ride would occur while the Maritime II was anchored just offshore of the location of the new ride.

Just offshore from where something had happened years ago that nobody wanted to talk about.

I'M DOING THIS for Bruce, Matt thought. His stepfather was seated in the front row. Although it was technically his company, he had trusted Matt with the presentation.

Matt stood just to the right of the three Hamilton siblings. Jack, the oldest, was in charge of rides at Starlight Point while his sister June handled shows and Evie took care of the hotel and the marina. Matt didn't know how much overlap there was, but he had noticed the three siblings stuck together like glue.

His own brother was there, too, seated right behind Bruce. Lucas had saved him from a painful conversation earlier by pretending that Jack wanted to see him.

It would have been a lousy question anytime, but being asked right in front of Caroline Bennett twisted the words like a knife in his gut. He wanted Caroline to think well of him. And he didn't want her opening an old can of worms that would, at the very least, hurt his stepfather's feelings and bring pain to his already weakened heart.

It wasn't his fault John Corbin's company had a disastrous ride to its credit. It wasn't John Corbin's fault the ride had been dogged with publicity bad enough to close it after one season.

Matt wanted to inherit the company without any scars or stains. Somehow, he'd hoped no one would make the connection between JC Construction and Bayside Construction, even though he'd known all along it would only be a matter of time.

Jack Hamilton had the attention of the guests and reporters as he built up to the unveiling of the ride diagrams, the announcement of the ride's names and the big reveal of the unusual double coaster. Every eye was on Jack. Except for one set of green eyes.

Caroline sat near the back, and her green dress stood out in the sea of white shirts. He was a fool. He'd been only milliseconds from telling her how beautiful she was before that meddling reporter popped into the conversation and dropped a bomb about his company's past.

Matt wondered how old he would have to be before he stopped trying to outrun the past and other people's mistakes. All he could do now was think about the future he had to build for himself, his mother and his brother. The only way to do that was hope his stepfather's heart held out long enough to see the end of the massive project that could be—had to be—Matt's crowning glory.

He tried to read Caroline's expression from a distance. Was it safer for him to steer clear of her or tell her the whole sad story of his uncle's broken spirit?

He wondered why she was so interested in that old ride. The story was clear. It was an accident that was never determined to be anyone's fault. The state inspectors had absolved the construction company and Starlight Point of guilt. The ride closed because of negative perception and diminished rider interest and was torn down.

His uncle had sold his business to his brother, but neither of them ever seemed to feel right about it. This had never been said out loud and no one talked about it, but the fact that John had moved away and started another business made Matt wonder. Bruce worked hard for years and made Bayside Construction a success, but his brother's recent death had seemed to reopen an old wound.

What did Caroline think she was going to find by digging around in ancient history?

CHAPTER EIGHT

WHY CAN'T NEWSPAPERS put all their old editions online? Caroline had discovered that the *Bayside Times* had digital editions available for only the last ten years. If she wanted to see the newspapers from the summer of 1985, she had two choices: public library or newspaper office.

The library was by far the easier option. Its website was inviting and gave clear directions to the archives on the upper floor. No appointment necessary. And she had to do *something* while she waited for her records request to arrive from the state agency.

On her Tuesday off, Caroline packed her laptop and notebook and drove to downtown Bayside. The Bayside City Library was in a historic building just steps from the water. It shared a block with a park, a gazebo and a convenient parking lot. As Caroline entered the stone building, she noted the graceful arch over the front door with the year 1879 carved in it.

This place held all the answers. She hoped.

In the third-floor archive, the librarian helped her sort through microfiche sheets—something she'd only seen on television shows and in pictures in her college textbooks. She focused the film reader and began to read two weeks' worth of articles from July 1985.

The front page of the *Bayside Times* the day after the accident had a picture, but the photograph wasn't helpful. It showed the ride entrance shrouded in darkness with a Closed sign.

The article described the accident, including several eyewitness accounts. All the witnesses interviewed were on the Loose Cannon at the time. No one on the midway or even the ride platform had seen what happened, and the actual riders were also unclear because of one important fact: the accident had occurred after dark.

The riders interviewed, four of them, said almost exactly the same thing. They felt a jerking or lurching sensation, heard a scream, and then the ride continued into the station. The riders all believed this had happened near the end of the ride as it approached the unloading platform.

The officials from Starlight Point had no comment. They all deferred to the state agency that was expected to send out inspectors the morning after the accident.

Caroline knew that Starlight Point had been sold to the Hamilton family at the end of that season, so it was no surprise that she didn't recognize the names of the publicity person or the ride supervisor.

Both Starlight Point and JC Construction had changed hands by the end of 1985. *Interesting.*

The saddest part of the article was the story of the twelve-year-old girl thrown from the train, possibly because she was the smallest person on the ride, who fell over twenty feet to the ground, and then died of her injuries a short time later at the local hospital.

Caroline was not surprised when she read the girl's name. Jenny Knight. The girl whose parents lived with her loss just down the street from Caroline's childhood home. The article also described one person who had a broken collarbone and possible dislocated shoulder from being jerked violently on the ride.

Caroline flipped to the rest of the article printed on an interior page of the paper, hoping she would find more pictures. Instead, there was only one more paragraph with quotations from the owner of Starlight Point, a man named Culbertson, who insisted that the park had a flawless safety record and guests would find all the other rides open and safe. Page two of the newspaper featured the small headline Maintenance Worker Dies at Starlight Point.

Here was the gold, she thought. The article explained that a maintenance worker had been accidentally electrocuted while working on a ride late at night. The three-paragraph story gave the man's name, George Dupont, and explained that he had failed to follow lockout procedure even though he'd worked there twenty years. The article included no speculation as to why the man was under the Loose Cannon so late at night just hours after the accident.

Didn't anyone else think it was one heck of a coincidence?

Caroline moved the microfiche reader to the next day of the *Bayside Times*. She expected to see a full report from the state agency with findings on what caused the accident. She also hoped to find more information about the ill-fated maintenance man.

Disappointment settled into her stomach. The article included a picture of men in hard hats checking the ride. When interviewed, the inspectors said there were no obvious indications of what caused the lurching the riders described. They saw nothing out of place, nothing mechanically wrong with the ride. The team of inspectors said they would complete a report, but the ride was cleared to reopen the next day.

The same edition had an update on the condition of the injured guests. The man with the shoulder injury had been treated and released from a local hospital.

The most surprising thing in the article was a paragraph about the deceased girl's father, who was nearly arrested for taking a swing at the Starlight Point spokesperson who went to the hospital to meet with the family in the hours after the accident. Although the girl's father was detained by hospital security, Starlight Point declined to press charges and the matter was dropped. Caroline tried to imagine the sweet, quiet, elderly gentleman she'd known threatening someone.

But the worst had happened to him. A senseless, horrific loss.

Caroline flipped through the next week's newspapers with a heavy heart. For day three after the accident, she found the obituary of George Dupont, but it did not include any details about the cause of death. For day seven, she found a follow-up on the report from the state agency, which labeled the cause of the accident inconclusive and noted that the ride was back in operation.

From day eight on, the *Bayside Times* did not mention the Loose Cannon accident—until Caroline inserted a new microfiche sheet and flipped to the September editions. In the middle of the month when the summer operating season had come to a close and the park's gates were shut, there was a lengthy front-page article about the future of Starlight Point.

The story explained that the Loose Cannon would be dismantled, and it rehashed the

July accident. No new details had emerged since the state agency had closed the case, and the cause of the accident was again labeled as undetermined. There was no mention of the company that had the contract to tear down the ride, but Caroline already knew its name. JC Construction, the builder and destroyer of the Loose Cannon.

Whatever her research turned up, she hoped Matt Dunbar would never have to tear down a ride he'd built as his uncle had.

He hadn't shared information with her, but she still respected how much he cared about his work. Caroline had never built anything larger than a birdhouse for an art project, but she imagined it would be demoralizing and devastating to have to knock down something that took a year to build.

Was that why John Corbin sold the company to his brother, Matt's stepfather? Was his enthusiasm for construction destroyed by the short life of the Loose Cannon?

The article continued inside the front page and included speculation that Starlight Point would be sold because the owner had an "opportunity" in another state. There was no timeline for the sale, other than a quote from an unnamed source saying it would happen before the next season. There was no potential buyer listed. As a privately owned business, Starlight Point was not required to file federal forms disclosing worth, so there was no information about the purchase or sale price.

"Are you finding everything you need?"

Caroline jumped. The librarian stood over her shoulder and had crept up so silently Caroline hadn't even known she was there.

"I'm fine," she said. "Thank you." The librarian glanced at Caroline's untouched paper and Caroline imagined it looked as if she wasn't finding anything worth writing down.

Which was close to the truth.

"I see you're reading about Starlight Point," the librarian said. "Any reason in particular?"

How much should she reveal to the archivist? Perhaps the older lady knew something useful.

"I'm interested in the history of the place," Caroline said. It was true, but not the whole truth.

"You might like to see a book on the history. We have one in our collection."

"You do?" Caroline feared it was too good to be true. "What years does the book include? Anything from the last thirty years?"

The librarian shook her head. "Sorry, it's all early history. Turn of the century to the mid-1950s. Beautiful black-and-white pictures of the Lake Breeze hotel being built, early photographs of the midway and the carousel. I could find it for you if you think it would be helpful at all."

Caroline wanted to remain in the good graces of the librarian, who was clearly enthusiastic about the old book and pictures. "I'd love to see it," she said.

"Be right back."

While the librarian consulted shelves of books on the other side of the room, Caroline skimmed through sheets of microfiche. She was looking for an article about the sale of Starlight Point, which she already knew happened that fall. A November issue of the *Bayside Times* provided the information she needed.

Starlight Point was sold for an undisclosed sum to Ford Hamilton, who was previously the general manager of the park. Culbertson indicated he had plans to move to Florida where he had an interest in a small family-owned theme park. Ford Hamilton expressed excitement about Starlight Point and his enthusiasm for the future.

End of story.

But it wasn't the end of the story. If Ford Hamilton was the general manager at the time of the accident, he had to know more about it than almost anyone else. Unfortunately, he had passed away several years before Caroline came to work at Starlight Point. How much more did his widow and children know about the accident? Caroline imagined it wouldn't be polite dinner conversation at a Hamilton family affair.

"Here's the book," the librarian said.

She must have the quietest shoes in the county. Caroline smiled and accepted the book.

"You can't check it out, but if you'd like a copy of any of the pages, just let me know and I'll put it on the document scanner."

Caroline surrendered her microfiche machine, gathered her notebook and found a comfortable chair by a window. She began leafing through the one-hundred-page book, which consisted primarily of pictures with detailed captions.

A three-page preface at the front gave a history of the peninsula that housed Starlight Point and information about early entrepreneurs who recognized that the unique location had possibilities for recreation. The book appeared to be professional and well researched. It was also far more interesting than she'd expected it to be.

She flipped past photos of old wooden roller coasters, long defunct according to the dates in the captions. Women in long dresses with pretty hats walking along the beach boardwalk in front of the hotel. Men in three-piece suits and hats riding the carousel. Families disembarking from the ferry that brought them across the bay or from cities along Lake Huron.

Parts of Starlight Point had hardly changed. She recognized the arcade building and enjoyed seeing the ballroom as it looked in 1945. Caroline wondered if the men pictured dancing with their local sweethearts were freshly home from the war. One of the men was tall and blond with a crew cut. He reminded her of someone who'd gotten under her skin far more than she'd expected.

Not that she'd expected to meet an interesting man at Starlight Point this summer.

What had Matt been about to say when the reporter interrupted them a few days ago on the boat cruise? Matt had said, "You look—"

How did he plan to finish that statement? You look hungry? You look as if you were only invited because your brother married well? You look out for pirates and warn me if you see any?

Or was it you look pretty? Beautiful?

It doesn't matter, Caroline thought as she paged through the book. She would never know the answer to that question, and she was beginning to think she'd never know what caused the Loose Cannon to lurch or the maintenance man to die.

If there was one thing Caroline could not stand, it was a mystery going unanswered.

Matt had had opportunities to tell her the Loose Cannon had been built by his uncle's company, and he'd deliberately concealed that fact—until the reporter blew the news open. Matt himself had said that his smiles were a cover concealing his worries.

What else was he hiding?

CHAPTER NINE

CAROLINE TRIED TO enjoy her morning on the beach. She smoothed out a towel on a lounge chair and settled in for girl talk with her artist friend Agnes. With a fresh breeze off the lake on the first day of July and a bag full of magazines, drinks and snacks on the sand between them, it should have been a relaxing morning on the Starlight Point beach. The hotel towered behind them and summer tunes poured from the speakers spaced along the boardwalk.

Agnes kept up a steady stream of chatter, but all Caroline could think about was her lack of answers on the Loose Cannon accident.

"Which is why I swore I would never date another artist," Agnes said.

Caroline propped herself on an elbow and turned a guilty expression to her friend.

"You weren't even listening," Agnes said.

"Sorry. Tell me again why artists are off your list of eligible bachelors." *I really should try harder at being a friend.*

"Because they get all wrapped up in their work and I feel like they're not even hearing me," Agnes said. She tossed a bottle of water at Caroline and wet drops of ice-cold condensation sprayed her. "Now are you ready for my story?"

"Ready."

"I met Lucas last year when we were freshmen, and I thought he was adorable in a brooding sort of way. We had two classes together, and we both worked in the art gallery for campus jobs."

"So you had a lot in common," Caroline said, attempting to prove she was immersed in the story this time around. "And you dated?"

"We sort of dated. Almost dated."

Caroline laughed. "How do you almost date?"

"You ask someone out and don't show up, even though the girl you asked was waiting at the campus pub and even bothered to put on lipstick."

"He stood you up?"

"Yep," Agnes said. She sprayed sunscreen on her legs and rubbed it in meticulously. "He said he got emotionally involved in a portrait he was drawing and went for a walk to clear his head."

"Do you believe his story?"

"You sound exactly like a cop when you talk that way."

"Good," Caroline said. "I'm practicing. So, believe him or not?"

Agnes sighed. "I believed him. Like I said, he was a brooding artist. It's one of the things I liked about him. And he showed me the portrait later. You should have seen it. I swear you could feel the passion rising right off the page."

Caroline tried to imagine passion rising off a piece of paper. She'd taken one art class in high school and decided it wasn't for her when a spin of the color wheel told her she had no sense of complementary colors. Police uniforms were uncomplicated. Black shirt, black pants, black shoes. She even had a drawer full of black socks.

"Who was in the portrait?"

"His father."

This was interesting. Caroline knew nothing about Matt's father, but she did know Matt and Lucas had a stepfather. She'd seen Bruce Corbin on the media cruise last week. He was pale, sat most of the time, didn't seem to eat or drink, and he let his stepson do all the talking. Was Matt not only in charge of the roller coaster build, but possibly the entire company?

"Lucas drew his own father wearing an orange prison jumpsuit in a cell wallpapered with dollar bills," Agnes said. "It was painful to look at. Lucas is a very good portrait artist, and you could see from the picture how much Lucas must resemble his dad. But the agony in every line of that drawing... I could hardly look at it."

Caroline leaned closer to her friend. "Why would he draw his father in jail?"

"Because that's where he is."

"What?"

"Lucas broke down and told me the whole story. He was only five when his dad—who was some kind of accountant—got caught stealing money and got a twenty-year sentence."

"Twenty years? That must have been a lot of money." Caroline had read about cases of embezzlement and other white-collar crimes in her criminal justice classes. Twenty years was a very long time.

Agnes shrugged. "I guess it was. I think it involved tax fraud, too. That's bad, right?"

"Yes. You're getting into the felony range. That may explain the twenty years."

"Either way, he went to jail, the cops raided their house, and Lucas ended up in a homeless shelter with his mom and his older brother."

Caroline felt a sick twist in her stomach. Of course the police had to raid the house. There was probably evidence inside. And all the criminal's assets were probably seized. But she imagined five-year-old Lucas, his distraught mother and his older brother facing that terrible thing. Did they stand in the yard and watch their home being searched and taped off? Weren't there any relatives to take them in?

"How old was his brother at the time? I think Matt's a few years older, right?" Caroline asked. She had guessed that she and Lucas were about the same age, and Matt seemed to be about the same age as her older brother, Scott. She pictured her older brother trying to shield her from sorrow and imagined it was much the same for Matt and his brother.

Agnes nodded. "Six years, I think."

How does an eleven-year-old boy feel when his father goes to jail and he loses everything except his mother and his little brother? Perhaps he feels like he has the world on his shoulders—or in the back of his dump truck. No wonder Lucas had drawn Matt that way. Tears stung Caroline's eyes.

"That's a sad story," she muttered, pretending to search for something in her beach bag so Agnes wouldn't see her shining eyes and pink face. "And his father must still have a few years left on his sentence."

"I guess."

"So, did you forgive Lucas after you heard this story and agree to another date with him?"

"Not exactly. Spring break came up, and then we were busy with finals. And then school was over and we both ended up here for the summer."

"And?"

"He seems really troubled, but he doesn't want to talk about it. Maybe it's the whole dad-in-jail thing. We're friends, but I don't know if it will go beyond that."

Caroline adjusted her sunglasses and reclined on her beach chair. "There's still plenty of summer left, so you never know."

"How about you?"

"Not interested in Lucas."

Agnes laughed. "You know what I mean. Have you met your summer romance yet?"

Caroline closed her eyes, and Matt's face came to her mind. His blond buzz cut framing a wide smile. Green eyes. What was he hiding behind that smile? Instead of drawing portraits immortalizing his childhood pain, did he turn his passion into blueprints and construction jobs?

She knew something about converting feelings into work; it was behind her quest for justice.

And, unfortunately, her current quest involved Matt's stepfamily.

"I'm not looking for summer romance," Caroline said. "I don't want to be the girl wearing lipstick and waiting at the bar."

Two hours later, after showering off sand and sunscreen, Caroline faced one of the toughest decisions of her life.

She didn't want to do it. Breaking the

rules went against everything she believed in. Justice and laws were the only defense against a crazy and unfair world. But what happened when the rules made it harder for people with good intentions?

Talking with Agnes at the beach had made her realize how loyal Matt must be to his stepfather and how incredibly unlikely it was that Matt would give her any real information.

She was up against a dead end. The Knight family deserved answers, and the Dupont family deserved justice. Frustratingly, nothing was coming easily.

Files at Starlight Point were missing.

The local newspaper was no help.

Reports from the state inspection agency might contain nothing, even if she waited weeks more for their arrival.

And she certainly wasn't getting any information out of Matt's family about the ride. She respected family loyalty, but she also knew that getting past that loyalty to the truth could be like breaking into a sealed vault.

She had to find a way into the vault.

Since giving up was not an option, Caroline faced the fact that she needed to take drastic measures. With just two hours before she needed to be at work, she walked to the Starlight Point personnel office, which was tucked into a concrete block building near the marina.

She had no business being there, and she was taking a major risk that could destroy her reputation and her future, but at this point, she had no choice.

"Hi, Lucy," Caroline said cheerily to the girl at the front desk.

"Not working today, Caroline?" The girl gestured to Caroline's T-shirt and shorts.

"Not yet. Doing a little paperwork for the chief before my shift starts. I'm trying to organize our files, and we've found there's a lot of overlap with yours whenever an employee ends up getting involved with the police department here." Caroline swallowed. The lies almost stuck in her throat, but she was already committed. "I just need to look at some ancient files to see if your records match up with ours."

Lucy rolled her eyes. "Boring stuff, huh?"

"You're telling me." Caroline waved a piece of paper. "I just have to check off that these records are here, and then we can stick them in deep storage over at the station. I'll just be a minute."

"Help yourself," Lucy said. "I have to hold down this desk, so I can't help you dig."

"I'll be fine," Caroline said.

Heart pounding, she breezed through the glass door that separated the personnel office from a dimly lit records room.

The files in this musty room were in alphabetical order by name instead of categorized by month and year. Luckily, Caroline knew exactly what name she was searching for as she pulled out the *D* drawer and located the file on George Dupont.

Score. Her fingers trembling with guilt and the fear of consequences if she got caught searching records she had no right to see, Caroline opened the file. She hadn't dared to bring a scanner, but she slipped her cell phone from her pocket and started taking pictures.

It was the first crime she had ever committed, but she believed it was necessary so that justice would eventually be served—if she didn't end up fired and humiliated.

The folder contained standard HR documents, such as his original handwritten employment application, papers certifying him as an electrician, notifications of salaries and raises. Twenty years' worth of records, all of which indicated his loyal service to Starlight Point. He was unmarried, had no children, and his mother was listed as next of kin and beneficiary. He'd begun as a summer worker and was the head of maintenance when he died.

Caroline flipped to the medical examiner's report. Death by electrocution. Confirmed cause of death with an autopsy. Closed case. It was a surprisingly long report, though, and maybe there was something to be gleaned from it.

She glanced over her shoulder to confirm she was alone.

The medical examiner's report included the full autopsy. She skimmed past details such as the contents of the deceased's stomach, location and description of scars, and other general health issues. She read the description of his clothing. Plaid shirt with snap closures. Jeans. A thick leather belt with an attached key ring. Athletic socks and shoes.

He wasn't wearing his maintenance uniform?

No name tag or employee identification badge was found on the body. Wasn't he on duty at the time of the accidental electrocution? If not, why was he there?

The contents of his pockets were also listed and photographed. A wallet with a license, an insurance card and twenty-seven dollars in cash. A set of car keys.

Caroline looked closely at the picture. 1985 was before the era of the electronic key fob. The small ring held a car door key and an ignition key, both labeled Chevrolet. He also had some change, a tissue and a broken bolt in the pocket of his pants. Nothing out of the ordinary. Caroline squinted at the picture of the broken bolt. A small number five was stamped on its face.

There was no smoking gun. Nothing to indicate that his death was anything other than the accident it had been labeled.

She looked again at the image of the dead man's body. Why was he wearing street clothes instead of his uniform? Did it mean anything at all? If he was off duty and had come in to work, perhaps he was off his game. It could make him careless enough to forget a safety procedure. Maybe he was in a hurry to get back to whatever he was doing with his time off.

It was a theory. And there must have been nothing to indicate foul play at the time of the accident, or certainly someone would have looked more closely. The man's family, the owner of Starlight Point, the Point police, even the local police. Someone would have asked questions.

Unless they had something to hide.

If anything had been hidden, it had been concealed well enough to remain out of sight for over thirty years. Her chances of finding it now were practically zero.

She thought about the fire that had killed her sister, Catherine. It was twenty years ago now. No one had ever been charged, and no one ever would be.

Caroline gripped the photo of the dead man and ran a finger over the surface. Was it too late for him, too? And what kind of ghosts would she be disturbing if she continued to ask questions?

"IT'S GETTING DARK," Matt said. "How long will they make you stand out here?"

Caroline started and swung around. He knew he wouldn't usually stand a chance sneaking up on her, but the scrambler ride across the way was flashing and beeping obnoxiously, allowing him to approach unnoticed.

"Until the park clears," she said.

"I thought you usually had the day shift."

"I do. But I switched with one of the other guys so he could have an evening free."

Matt took off his hard hat and ran a hand over his hair. Since the afternoon media cruise, he'd wanted an opportunity to talk to Caroline about his family's connection to the Loose Cannon.

He knew how it looked. She'd brought it up several times, and he'd pretended not to know anything. The truth was, he didn't know much. He only knew how much it hurt his stepfather's and his uncle's feelings whenever it came up. He was so accustomed to it being an off-limits subject that he found it hard to talk about.

He'd found it strange that his stepfather's company had bid on the job for the new coaster at Starlight Point. Was it an opportunity for redemption as the pushy reporter had suggested?

He'd been thinking about approaching Caroline, and when he discovered she was still on duty it seemed like a perfect chance. He had no idea what she knew about the Loose Cannon or why she was asking questions. It was risky, getting close to a woman who asked too many questions, but Starlight Point was a small world. He couldn't avoid her forever.

"Date?"

"I didn't ask why he wanted the night off," Caroline said, confusion furrowing her brow.

"I mean…would you consider a coffee date with me?"

Although there were thousands of artificial lights along the midway and emanating from the rides and attractions, it was semidark along the construction fence where Caroline kept her usual post. He wished he could see her face clearly right now to judge whether she was about to say yes or arrest him for harassing an officer of the law.

"It's too late for coffee. I'd never get to sleep tonight."

"Welcome to my life. When this project is done in ten months, I plan to sleep for ten years."

"Then who would run your company?"

That question was too close to the heart. Would Bruce still be alive next summer? And what would be the fate of Bayside Construction either way?

"It's not a one-man show," he said.

"It looks that way to me."

"Well, it isn't." He spoke quickly and wished his tone wasn't that of a car door slamming.

"If it's not all on your shoulders, why can't you sleep at night?"

Matt jammed his hard hat back on his head. No matter how interesting he found Caroline. No matter how much he wanted to see what made her tick. No matter how pretty she was in that green dress on that cruise, it was dangerous and difficult trying to figure out why she was interested in the Loose Cannon and his family's company. It was a tough chapter in his family's past, and he didn't want her opening that book, but trying to outwit her was obviously pointless.

"You take your job seriously, Caroline,"

he said. For some reason, using her name for the first time felt personal. She moved a little so her face was lit up by a beam from the fence's lighting. Judging from her wide eyes, he had her attention. "So you certainly understand why I take mine seriously."

"I do."

Matt breathed. Maybe this would be okay. He could take her out for a late-night beverage—not coffee—and maybe she would tell him why she kept asking questions that made him uncomfortable.

"Why do bolts have numbers stamped on them?" she asked.

What? Was he so bad at asking a girl out that she reverted to construction questions? He had no idea where she was coming from, and the only way he could answer the question was with the simple truth.

"It's their grade. It indicates the strength of the bolt."

"Is five a good grade?"

"Depends what it's being used for."

Caroline flicked a glance at the construction area. "What kind will you use on the new ride?"

Maybe taking Caroline out for a beverage

was a really bad idea. He already doubted everything about his life and, if she began to question the few things he was sure he understood, he wouldn't sleep for a thousand years.

"We'll use what it says on the construction blueprints."

"What does it say?"

Matt huffed out a long breath. The heck with coffee or anything else. He might as well stay up all night working.

"It depends on the part of the ride. Non-weight-bearing applications can handle a lower grade of bolt, but we use grade eight for high-stress applications."

"Are the number eights bigger?"

Matt shook his head. "Stronger. The numbering system is its strength and indicates the amount of force it would take to sheer it off."

He'd spent a lot of time wondering what his father was thinking when he made those disastrous criminal decisions years ago. He'd been wondering lately what was going through his stepfather's mind and his decision about the future of his company. But right now, Matt would give almost anything to know what Caroline was driving at with her out-of-left-field questions about bolts.

"I'm not off work until midnight and I have to be back at seven, so a…beverage date…isn't going to work out tonight."

Maybe it was for the best.

"Another time," Matt said, expecting it would be the easy out she was probably looking for.

"Why are you asking me out?"

"I thought we could talk," he said. The truth was the truth. "By now you certainly know about my stepfamily's history."

She nodded. "Do you know what caused the accident on the Loose Cannon?"

"No."

She stared at him as if she was trying to read his face for lies. He couldn't lie even if he wanted to. As far as he knew, no one was certain what caused the Loose Cannon to toss out a rider and injure others. He knew what everyone else did. The investigation was inconclusive, the ride closed at the end of the season and his family preferred never to talk about it.

"I have to teach self-defense classes for Virginia Hamilton's summer project tomorrow

night, but you could show up if you want.
Then you could tell me everything you know."

Matt swiped a hand over his eyes. How
could he talk to her about the Loose Cannon without revealing it all—everything that
was in his heart and mind?

CHAPTER TEN

ON THE FIRST night of STRIPE classes in the ballroom at the arcade, the Hamilton family was there in full force. Virginia, Jack, June and Evie welcomed the two hundred seasonal and year-round employees who'd ventured out for the first night. A photographer from the publicity department was there, waiting with her camera and tablet.

What have I gotten myself into? Caroline had attended classes the previous year and listened to her brother extol the virtues of fire safety. She also knew, in theory, that she would lead the group of police officers and volunteers who would demonstrate self-defense techniques to every Starlight Point employee from the lifeguards to the cotton candy sellers. But she hadn't grasped the scale of the project until she surveyed the large group for the first of ten nights of classes.

Thick mats covered a section of the floor and rows of chairs contained the night's first group of trainees. True to her word, Virginia had secured volunteers from the Starlight Point police force and some from Bayside.

No matter how many helpers she had, though, Caroline felt the weight of the job on her shoulders. She had prepared a speech with examples and tips. Had worked up a lesson plan to fill the ninety minutes with useful knowledge and practical hands-on techniques. She hoped the skills would some-day help someone out of a tough situation—or help them avoid it.

"I always feel young again when I see all the young people lined up eager to learn," Virginia said. She stood near the edge of the stage with Caroline while her children officially welcomed people and showed them to their seats. "I remember when I was their age and I thought all I'd get out of my summer job was a paycheck." She laughed. "Boy, was I wrong."

Caroline smiled. "You met your husband here, right?"

"Yes. And plenty of other people have met their spouses here, too. I was definitely wrong when I thought I'd quickly forget about my summer loading roller coasters in the heat. I've heard from so many people over the years that working here sticks with you."

"Do you still keep in touch with the friends you made that first summer?"

"Some of them. Some still live in the area and I see them here on occasion with their kids and grandkids."

"Happy memories," Caroline commented. She was nervous about teaching the self-defense course even though she had done so well in college she was asked to be the assistant instructor for two succeeding courses. She'd even done a small course at the local library for senior citizens.

"Happy memories for almost everyone," Virginia said. "I have only one friend who won't ever come here, even though she still lives in Bayside."

"Why not?"

"She blames herself for something that, I'm sure, wasn't her fault."

"That's a shame," Caroline said. Was this about the Loose Cannon? Although fascinated, Caroline wondered why Virginia was telling her this story.

"It's always a shame when someone hauls around blame for something that's not her fault," Virginia said pointedly.

Because her brother had married into the Hamilton family, the entire family was aware of the sad story of her sister Catherine's death.

Virginia meant well, but Caroline couldn't talk about her sister right now. She cleared her throat and scanned the attendees to take her mind off her family's tragedy.

She recognized a number of the seasonal employees. From her post on the midway, she saw dozens of them troop past every day. She also lived in a dorm housing police officers, dancers, balloon sellers, ride attendants. They were friends she hoped to stay in touch with all her life.

Caroline imagined Virginia and her friends enjoying a sunny, youthful summer thirty years ago. Everyone deserved happy memories. That was one of the reasons for her class—teach people to take care of themselves and be smart. Think fast. Use your instincts. The very skills she wanted to cultivate in herself.

And paying attention when someone is about to hand you a clue to a mystery you're investigating.

"What does your friend blame herself for?" Caroline asked.

"She was working on the Loose Cannon the night of the accident. They never could figure out what caused the accident, so there was a rumor floated that it was employee error," Virginia said. She shook her head. "Some people said the cars were loaded wrong."

"Do you believe that?"

"No. We had good training back then. Not as good as it is now, but still adequate. I don't believe any of my friends were careless in loading those cars. There was a procedure in place and we followed it, no questions asked. It was drilled into our heads."

"But there was a formal investigation after the accident," Caroline said. "They would have certainly interviewed the workers. Wouldn't a ride operator error have come to light then?"

Virginia nodded. "That's the mysterious part. No one knew what had happened. It was dark, and nothing seemed out of the ordinary. The ride operators weren't officially blamed, but the suspicion hung over their heads anyway."

Caroline watched two blond men take seats in the front row. Lucas Dunbar was an employee and required to attend, but Matt was a contractor. He certainly didn't have to be here. Was he here because she had invited him?

"Maybe the ride had a mechanical error no one knew about," Caroline said, trying to keep her thoughts on Virginia's story while she watched Matt scan the area until he found her. He nodded, smiled. He had such a nice smile.

"They said there was nothing wrong with the ride, even though it was a new one."

"Not faulty construction, being new?" Caroline prodded.

"No. They went all over that thing the next day and came up with not one piece of steel out of place."

Perhaps the report for which she checked her post office box every day would have more details, but officially the construction company had been exonerated, the ride mechanics not held accountable.

Was it possible that the employees running the ride had been careless, despite Virginia's insistence they weren't? They were, after all, her friends. Could she be turning a blind eye? And if one of her friends wouldn't come near Starlight Point after thirty years had passed, did it mean she felt guilty about something?

"I only tell you this old story because I want you to understand that I feel our employees are all our family members. I want them to have wonderful memories of their time here like I have," Virginia said. She laid a hand on Caroline's arm and leaned closer, a smile lighting her face. "And if they learn how to gouge out an attacker's left eyeball, too, that's just icing on the cake."

Caroline laughed and turned her attention to the crowd of people listening to Jack as he explained the history of the program and reminded them to present their certificate of attendance to the personnel office. She tried to keep her mind on her lesson plan and mentally rehearse her safety speech, but her attention kept returning to the occupants of the front row.

Matt and Lucas Dunbar. She highly doubted either one of them needed self-defense classes. With their height and broad shoulders, they probably didn't feel vulnerable when they walked down a deserted street at night. Probably didn't check under their cars in dark parking lots or shine a flashlight in the back seat before they got in.

But they were vulnerable in other ways.

She hadn't stopped thinking about her friend Agnes's story about Lucas's portrait, and she couldn't help but imagine their young faces as their father was stuffed into a police car. Did they go to visit him in jail? Send him cards on Father's Day?

The two brothers had endured a lot when they were far too young. So had she and her brother, Scott.

Perhaps that's why Matt was so desperate to be a success. He needed a family legacy he could be proud of, his stepfather's company, instead of his father's disgrace and imprisonment. Although Caroline had begun to suspect Matt was covering up something involving the Corbin family and the construction of the Loose Cannon, Virginia had given her something to think about.

If all the reports said the construction of the ride was not to blame, they were probably right. And maybe she should give a man with a kind smile, green eyes and the whole world in the back of his truck more of a chance.

AFTER ONLY FIVE minutes of Caroline's instructions on how to avoid physical confrontation if possible and then meet it head-on if necessary, Matt was convinced she was not someone who would back down from a fight. He just hoped she had no intentions of fighting with him about anything—especially the Loose Cannon.

He admired the way she stood, shoulders straight, no nervous fidgeting. She was one of the most confident people he'd ever met. As he watched her command the audience, he realized it was one of the first things he'd noticed about her the night she'd held him in her flashlight's beam. The memory spread warmth through his chest.

He couldn't deny the dozens of times he'd thought of her. Or looked for her outside his fence. Or wondered if she was on duty. Or what she did when she wasn't.

Caroline gave a general lecture about being aware of one's surroundings and avoiding high-risk situations. She cautioned the younger workers—most of them about her own age, Matt thought—about safety on campuses. He wondered if she'd felt safe on her college campus and even now in her dorm room. Matt swallowed. He wanted Caroline to be safe wherever she went.

After her initial speech, Caroline divided the group, directing participants to the cushioned mats where one of her colleagues waited. It was time for the practical, hands-on training that Matt had been looking forward to most. Although he'd found listening to Caroline far more interesting than he'd expected.

Matt was first out of his chair, certain he wanted to be in Caroline's group. His brother followed him, along with at least a dozen girls who'd chosen the only female police officer's group.

He didn't know if the ladies in attendance felt more comfortable with a female instructor, but he had no intention of partnering with any of them. He and his brother could attempt to take each other down, for safety's sake, of course.

Although they were both the same few inches upward of six feet, Matt had construction muscle whereas Lucas weighed a good twenty pounds less. They'd backyard-wrestled a few times, but by the time they were equal enough in size to make it a fair fight, they were also old enough to know better.

They stood in a circle, waiting. Caroline kicked off her heavy black shoes, revealing neat black socks. No holes. Matt hoped she wouldn't require everyone to remove their shoes. Were his socks clean? Was he wearing the pair with a hole right at the end of his big toe? He had no idea what his brother's socks looked like. They'd probably have paint on them.

"You can leave yours on if you want," she said, tossing her shoes to the edge of the mat. "I just took mine off so I'm less likely to leave a mark on someone."

Some of the students exchanged nervous glances at the prospect of physical pain. His brother shot him a quick elbow and whispered, "She's looking at you."

Caroline was, indeed, looking at Matt. Her lips curved with a hint of a smile. He felt his heart stumble a moment on its way to the next beat.

"Sorry to ask, but I need a volunteer to help me out," Caroline said, still keeping him in her sights.

If Caroline asked him to push her police car ten miles at that moment, he would have done it. He stepped forward into the circle and everyone saw him. There was no turning back.

"Before you volunteer, though, I should warn you," Caroline said. "You might be sore tomorrow."

Matt laughed, grabbed his younger brother's shoulders and shoved him into the circle, attempting to trade places with him. Lucas elbowed Matt hard and ducked out of his grip.

"Nice evasion," Caroline told Lucas. "But I can still give you some pointers."

Lucas faded back and Matt stood in the middle. "I'm your volunteer," he said. "But you have to take it easy on me or I'll have to give my crew the day off tomorrow while I lick my wounds."

"Trust me," Caroline said. "You've easily got eighty pounds on me."

Matt relaxed his shoulders. It was probably more like a hundred pounds. Caroline was maybe five foot five and so slender he wondered how she could defend herself. What made her choose a career as a police officer? He'd noticed her diligence and passion for the job, but was there a powerful motivating force? Something in her past?

Matt vividly remembered his first encounter with police from his childhood. Maybe Caroline had a positive experience somewhere along the way. Her brother was a firefighter, so perhaps public safety was in their blood. He'd love a chance to ask her about it.

"Which is why, ladies, I want to show you how to get the advantage even with a much larger opponent," Caroline added.

Matt laughed. "Not sure I like the sound of that."

"Lesson one," Caroline said. "Pressure points. You can apply serious pain if you know where to press. It won't cause permanent damage if you do it right, but it will certainly discourage an attacker."

Matt drew a long breath.

"Remember, your goal is not to cause harm unless you have to. Your goal is to give yourself a chance to get away."

Facing Caroline, Matt tried for an expression of cheerful cooperation.

"Ready?" Caroline asked. She raised one eyebrow and smiled a little. "I'm sorry in advance. If you want, I can just tell people where the pressure points are, but it's more effective to show them."

"Go ahead. I'm tougher than I look."

"You're a good sport." Caroline put her hand on Matt's shoulder and he did his best not to flinch. "Right here," she said. She dug two fingers into the muscle near his neck and Matt felt his knees soften. He heard his brother laugh when he nearly fell to the mat.

"Sorry," Caroline said. She rubbed the sore spot with the heel of her hand. "It'll feel better in just a minute."

"Wow," said a young girl still wearing her sweeper uniform.

"I know," Caroline said. "Wow. And in that moment when all he was thinking about was the excruciating pain, I could easily have started running and gained ground. See what I'm saying?"

"That's amazing," the girl added.

"Not exactly what I was thinking," Matt complained.

In response, Caroline used her fingers to continue massaging the pain out of his shoulder. She kept one hand on his other shoulder, and the heat sank into his tired muscles.

"I'm completely at your mercy," he murmured.

Caroline leaned close and whispered in his ear. "You can get up anytime you want."

Her lips on his ear caused gooseflesh to sweep over his neck. Caroline had to notice it when he rolled his head in a circle. She smoothed her warm palm over his neck.

"I never want to get up."

As Caroline laughed, stepped back and offered her hand to pull him up, he tried to remember the last time a woman had touched him with such tenderness. But he couldn't.

CHAPTER ELEVEN

"I OWE YOU, absolutely owe you, for letting me abuse you in the name of personal safety," Caroline said. "Name your favorite late-night food, and I'm buying."

"Now?"

"I'm wide awake after that class and I have to fuel up because I'm teaching another class tomorrow night. And the next night. And the next."

"You'll be run ragged."

Caroline shrugged. "I love it. If I ever get tired of being a police officer—which I doubt—I can always teach at the police academy. Assuming I get in and assuming I graduate."

"You will," Matt said.

"I just need the recommendation of the police chief here."

"Which I'm sure you already have."

Caroline hoped she already had it. What

would the chief think if he knew how far she'd taken her private investigation of the Loose Cannon incident?

She'd made a records request from the state, taken a trip to the library and asked questions of anyone who would talk—including Virginia Hamilton. Those were all innocent curiosity, but if he found out about her unauthorized snooping in personnel records, there was no way the chief could let it go. She would deserve whatever punishment she got, even if it destroyed her dreams.

"I hope so," she said when Matt seemed to be waiting for her answer.

They were alone. All the employees, including Matt's brother, had already left. Many of them were going straight to their dorms, but some left in groups, probably with plans to visit the local bars and clubs.

Matt rubbed his eyes with the heels of both hands.

"I'm sorry," she said. He looked too tired to go out for a late-night meal.

"I'm not. If showing everyone how embarrassingly fast I'll succumb to pain helps somebody out in the future, it was worth it," he said. He raised an eyebrow and grinned.

"Of course I'll tell my crew I took it like a man."

"Not about that—although I tried to take it easy on you. I mean I'm sorry I didn't consider the fact that you'll be back here at dawn working on the site. You probably want to go home and get some sleep."

Matt smiled. "Remember the first night we met?"

How could she forget? A handsome man in a hard hat was the last person she'd expected to find on a trespassing call. He'd surprised her in many ways since that night almost two months ago.

"Of course," she said. She sat on the edge of the stage in the ornate ballroom and tied her shoes.

"I think that was the last time I got any sleep."

Caroline laughed. "Don't tell me you actually slept in that tent on the Western Trail."

"Must have been the fresh air. Even though I did spend some time worrying about lions."

"Sorry about that. I have a wicked streak."

"I noticed. It's one of the things I like about you."

One of the things?

She picked up her bag and headed for the panel of light switches along the wall of the ballroom. The floor mats were staying for the ten-day string of classes as there were no other scheduled events.

Matt followed her to the wall and leaned on it while she turned off the switches one at a time. Darkness blotted out sections of the ballroom until there was only the space where she and Matt stood.

She paused, her finger on the switch. Did she want to be alone in the dark with Matt? She had nothing to fear physically. If his general sweetness wasn't proof enough, he now knew for certain she could take him down with one hand.

It was a different kind of danger. They stood face to face and at least five seconds of silence passed. He leaned closer to her, only inches, but it was enough. He was going to kiss her. And what would she do?

She considered it for a sliver of a second, but he rocked back on his heels and added distance between them.

"Burgers and fries," he said. "Maybe a beer."

Nervous laughter escaped Caroline's throat. "Not for me."

"You'd prefer pizza or something else?"

"I meant the beer. I turn twenty-one next week."

"Then I'll owe you one," Matt said.

Caroline flicked off the last light switch. They were back on solid ground now, but she still wondered what a kiss from Matt would have been like. She began walking toward the glass doors illuminated by the midway lights from outside.

"I believe I owe you tonight. So burgers and fries it is."

"Do you want to get something here at the Point or go elsewhere?"

Caroline considered the question as she closed and locked the ballroom doors behind them. She pocketed her work keys and began walking along the midway as she considered Matt's question.

The loudspeakers blaring summer music combined with the roller coaster noise made talking difficult. She appreciated the respite as she weighed her dining options with a man she found more intriguing than she wanted to.

If they ate at the burger-and-fry stand on the midway, it would be casual. Friendly. Just coworkers eating for survival. It would also be short-lived as the restaurant workers were probably already looking forward to cleaning their grills and going home. She could buy him a quick meal, make conversation for thirty-seven minutes and send him packing. It was a safe choice.

However, there was also a very good chance one of her colleagues would walk by and see her sharing a meal with Matt. She wanted the other police officers to see her as all business, no vulnerability. They might ask questions she didn't want to answer.

On the other hand, if they left the Point... in a car...and went to a place that served food and beer...

That sounded like a date.

Maybe if she drove her police-auction car she'd feel less vulnerable.

"Let's go somewhere else," she said decisively.

"Great. I'll drive."

"That's okay. We can take my car. I may even let you try out the spotlight since I owe you and all."

Matt paused midstep. "I have to confess something, and I'm asking for mercy in advance."

"Do you have a problem riding in a former police car?" Caroline kept her tone light but wondered if Matt had lingering distrust of police officers after what happened to his father. Would she ever know him well enough to ask about the day his dad went to jail?

"No," Matt said. "It's about my truck."

"Don't tell me your truck is illegally parked somewhere and you have to move it."

"How the heck did you guess that?"

"I'm an officer of the law. It's my job to sniff out crime."

Matt laughed. "I'll buy dessert if you'll look the other way when you see my truck is parked in the reserved restaurant spaces in the marina lot. I was desperate to find a spot because I didn't want to be late to class."

"No way," Caroline said, shaking her head. "You're getting a ticket. And then you're driving on our date."

Caroline was almost certain her heart stopped. Why did she open her big mouth and use the word *date*?

They were walking past the kiddie rides on the midway. Only a few of the old-fashioned cars were on the track, and streetlights shone brightly causing the rustling leaves on the old cottonwoods to cast shadows on the ground.

Matt waved to a little boy driving past. The boy took one hand off the wheel for a quick wave and then got back to the serious work of driving his mom around the track.

"I'll take that deal," Matt said.

"I was only kidding."

He stopped directly under a streetlight and Caroline could see his expression. Usually jovial, Matt looked serious.

"About which part?"

"The ticket," Caroline said quickly, not wanting to discuss the *date* word she'd tossed into the conversation. "The restaurant is closed anyway this late at night."

They continued walking toward the marina gate, sharing the wide concrete midway with hundreds of park guests who were staying until the lights went out on the coasters. Matt's hand brushed Caroline's as they moved aside for a group of teenagers. When the group had gone by and the midway opened up, Matt continued to walk so close to Caroline she felt his shirt touch her bare upper arm.

They exited the park and crossed the Outer Loop road. Caroline's dorm and assigned parking space were only a dozen yards off, but she turned away from them and walked side by side with Matt toward his truck.

"Just give me a minute," Matt said when he clicked his doors unlocked. "I don't usually have passengers."

He opened the passenger side door and picked up a first aid kit, a pair of safety glasses, a hammer and a flashlight and deposited them in a bin in the bed of his truck. He returned and took a heavy orange traffic cone off the floor, tossed it in the bed and then took a roll of shop towels out of the glove box.

"It's probably clean, but you never know," he said as he scrubbed the vinyl seat with a thick blue towel.

"These aren't my finest clothes," Caroline said. She considered asking for ten minutes so she could dash over to her dorm room and change into something nicer than black pants and a black T-shirt with the Starlight

Point Police Department logo on the chest. It was not exactly a date outfit.

Matt wore jeans and a green T-shirt. His shirt had Bayside Construction and his name embroidered over the chest pocket. On the back, it said Safety First in large white letters.

They looked like two people just leaving work and having a friendly burger together. Caroline resolved not to change her clothes. It was easier to keep the night casual while wearing casual clothing.

"Ready," Matt said. He held the door open while she got in and then he closed it.

Caroline had five seconds to process the inside of his truck while he circled around to his door. Industrial vinyl seats. Dusty dashboard, probably from construction sites. Matt seemed like the kind of guy who would keep the windows rolled down most of the time. The smell was industrial without being offensive. The seat belt worked.

Matt slid in next to her and put his key in the ignition. The only thing between them on the vinyl seat was a clipboard with a hard hat on top. She didn't have to inspect the hat.

She knew it said Dunbar in black marker on the side.

"You should tell me where we're going before I start the engine. It's loud. Sorry."

"Do you have a favorite place for burgers?"

"I'm a big fan of the Big Bayside Burger they serve at the Pony Express."

The Pony Express was, technically, a restaurant. Located just past the other end of the Point Bridge, the establishment also offered an arcade and bowling alley. One of Caroline's police colleagues who happened to have twin sons had recently told her about a children's birthday party he'd endured there—complete with pizza, game tokens and bumper bowling.

In addition to the family-friendly end of the facility, the Pony Express was also locally known for its bar where patrons could imbibe while enjoying offtrack horse betting. Gambling seemed risky enough without adding alcohol, but the state laws had loosened considerably in the past few years.

"I've never been there," she said. "But I'll take your word for it."

Matt was right about his truck. As he accelerated out of the parking lot, he observed the speed limit and the hand signals of the traffic employee, but the diesel engine still roared and discouraged conversation.

"The air conditioning doesn't work," Matt said, "but I could roll down my window if you're too warm."

It was a balmy summer night, but thousands of insects swirled under the street lamps on the bridge.

"I'd risk a bug in the eye if you want," Matt said.

"No way. You're driving, and I think you've suffered enough tonight. I'm fine."

"You're quiet."

"What?" Caroline shouted, exaggerating the word and putting a hand behind one ear.

Matt laughed and gave up talking until they pulled into the Pony Express parking lot. Caroline opened her door at the same time Matt did, eliminating the question of whether or not he would have come around and opened it for her. She didn't need to test him. And she was certainly capable of handling the job herself.

"Does it bug the cop in you that there's gambling here?" Matt asked as they walked toward the entrance. The door was over-shadowed by a colorful neon sign shaped like a field of racing horses.

Caroline shrugged. "It's stupid but legal, just like a lot of other things."

Matt held open the restaurant's door. "Eating heavy fried food late at night probably falls into that category, too."

"I'll take that chance."

They found a table between the bar and the bowling alley and opened their laminated menus. A waitress wearing a Pony Express T-shirt and khaki shorts stopped by their table.

"Start you off with something from the bar?" she asked.

Caroline was tempted to order a beer just to see if they would check her identification, but she suppressed her police persona. She was here to say thank you to Matt for volunteering at her self-defense course. Maybe if she was very nice to him, he'd come back for the next nine nights. She glanced up and met his eyes. Was he wondering what he should order?

"Lemonade for me," Caroline said.

"Make that two," Matt added.

The waitress left, promising to return in a few minutes to take their orders.

"I wouldn't care if you had a beer," Caroline said. "You'd be under the limit if you had just one."

Matt lifted one shoulder and let it fall. "Maybe I'll wait and have one with you next week. Which day is your birthday?"

"July 12. The day after I finish the STRIPE classes."

"I remember my twenty-first birthday. My friends wanted me to do things I'd either fail to remember or live to regret the rest of my life."

"And did you?"

He shook his head. "It was exam week at the end of my junior year. I was taking extra classes—extra hard classes—so I could eventually graduate early. And there was no way I could risk a hangover."

"So you stayed home and studied."

He nodded. "My friends weren't impressed, but they weren't the ones paying my tuition. My stepfather has been very generous to me and Lucas, but he has a right to expect we won't abuse it."

"I believe I saw your stepfather on the media cruise."

"He was there, yes."

"And he owns Bayside Construction?"

Caroline already knew the answer to the question. Despite her resolve to back off on the construction angle of the Loose Cannon, she wanted to see what Matt would say.

"Ready to order?" the waitress asked as she set down two glasses of lemonade.

Matt waited for Caroline to order first, and she selected a chicken-and-fries basket. She was not surprised when he ordered the Big Bayside Burger, a double-stacked sandwich with bacon and barbecue sauce. Caroline imagined how many calories a man on a construction site burned off every day.

"Yes," Matt said as soon as the waitress left. "Bruce owns the company. I believe you heard what the reporter said on the cruise. He bought it from his brother after the failure of the Loose Cannon."

Matt stated the situation matter-of-factly and left Caroline nothing to ask. If he had anything to hide, it certainly didn't look that way.

"We don't talk about it much in our family," he added.

"Why not?"

Matt sipped his drink and set it carefully on the cardboard coaster. She could practically see him weighing his words. She wished she could take the question back.

"Maybe I'm wrong," Matt said. "But it seems to me that every family has something they just don't talk about."

Caroline had her fingers around her lemonade glass, but she didn't pick it up to drink. It already felt as if she had swallowed an ice cube that chilled her all the way down. She knew far too well what it was like to avoid a painful family topic.

MATT HAD SEEN Caroline's determined expression, her humorous expression and her everyday I'm-serious-about-my-job expression. But he had not seen the look he now saw on her face.

Her fair skin had paled at least two shades, she looked down instead of meeting his eyes, and he would swear he saw her lip tremble. What had happened? Was it the mention of family skeletons in the closet? He had to change the subject.

"So tell me about your classes. Criminal justice major, right?"

Caroline nodded. "I finished my bachelor's degree in just three years, and now I'm ready to start using it."

"I can understand that. I thought I'd never finish college and actually start work."

"You have a master's?"

"Yes. University of Michigan. Bachelor's in engineering, master's in construction engineering."

A faint smile returned to Caroline's face and erased the odd look he'd seen a few moments ago. "So you get the hard jobs and that's why you wander around at night."

"I'm willing to take on the tough jobs. It's what I always wanted. Even with a degree, though, I wish I knew as much as my stepdad. He has a lifetime of experience. So did my uncle."

"Did?"

"My uncle passed away over the winter."

Matt could have sworn he saw Caroline adding up that information and placing it in a category in her brain.

"Does Bruce have any other children?

Any stepbrothers or sisters who might want to take over his business?"

"No. Just me and Lucas to carry on the family legacy."

"Maybe you could share it, like your stepfather and his brother did."

Matt wondered whether Caroline was asking because she was interested in getting to know him or because she wanted to know more about whatever happened on the Loose Cannon thirty years ago. She certainly loved to ask questions, but he didn't know how much he wanted to answer.

"They never shared it," Matt said flatly.

"I wonder if I could talk to your stepfather sometime," Caroline said. "I've read about the Loose Cannon roller coaster, and I'd love to talk to someone who was there at the time."

"He wasn't there."

"But his brother was. Maybe—"

"No," Matt cut her off. "Like I said, it's a painful topic in our family and my stepfather isn't in the best of health."

"Haven't you ever wondered why no one wants to talk about it?"

Matt took a deep breath. He had no intention of answering that question, even if he knew what to say.

Yes, he'd wondered. He'd even heard the rumors about the maintenance man who died later that night. He'd heard speculation that it was murder committed by the father of the dead girl, but the man had been cleared at the time. As far as Matt knew, there was never any evidence it was even a murder. It was a tainted, messy affair all around.

"Our food's here," he said, relieved to see the waitress approaching with two red plastic baskets of steaming food. He was starving, having skipped dinner to finish setting some steel beams. He waited while Caroline squirted half a bottle of ketchup on her fries and chicken strips.

She glanced up and caught him staring. "I love ketchup," she said with a grin.

"So you do have a weakness. I wondered."

"I have plenty of those," she said.

"Aside from doughnuts with maple frosting and a dogged thirst for justice, what else do you have a weakness for?"

Caroline paused, french fry in hand. "My thirst for justice isn't a weakness."

"Sorry. I have a dogged belief in the laws of engineering, but it can be a pain being such a worrier. I thought maybe you had the same problem."

"I don't."

"No matter what it takes to make someone face his punishment, even if there's collateral damage, you'd do it."

"Of course. What's the alternative?"

Matt took a big bite of his sandwich, glad it would take him a long time to chew so he didn't have to come up with an answer.

He knew what it was like to be collateral damage from someone else's crime. Caroline couldn't possibly know about his father's imprisonment, but it wouldn't matter if she did. He imagined her stoically leading his dad to court in handcuffs, righteous in her mission to uphold the law.

What would she think of him if she found out he was the son of a man doing time? More important, why was she so sure there were secrets left to be found about a roller coaster three decades in the past?

"What's your weakness?" Caroline asked.

I'm a desperate man, he thought. *Desperate to make this project work, desperate to forget about my childhood, desperate to se-cure my future and that of my family. What could that desperation make me do? How far will I go to achieve those goals?*

Caroline laughed and Matt looked up sharply. "You look like I just asked you to rob a bank and you're trying to think of a way to turn me down," she said.

"I wouldn't rob a bank." He said it casually, but he wondered what she would think if she knew his father had committed a similar crime.

"Me, neither," she said. "Too much paperwork."

Matt smiled and rolled his shoulders, trying to shrug off his serious thoughts. He was having a late-night dinner with a lovely and interesting woman. When was the last time he'd done that? Too long ago.

"You know," Caroline said, "you're one of the few people I know who can manage to smile and still look worried." She pointed with her index finger. "You get a little line right between your eyebrows, and it always makes me wonder what you're thinking about."

"Do you ever turn off your investigator light?" he asked.

"No."

"You were probably the kid who got to the bottom of stolen lunches and missing pairs of scissors in school."

She smiled. "Always. I even set up a camera in the backyard one summer to see what animal was living under my parents' shed."

"Groundhog?"

She wrinkled her nose, and it made her look quirky and vulnerable. "Worse. It was a skunk."

"And you caught him on camera?"

"Sadly, no. Our family dog sniffed him out. My brother let him out after dark one night and we heard all kinds of yipping from the backyard. Scott opened the back door without thinking and the dog came barreling in."

"Did he get sprayed?"

Caroline nodded. "Right in the face. And he rolled all over the living room carpet to try to get the smell out. My mother washed that dog with everything you can imagine. Tomato soup, dish soap, expensive shampoo from the vet. He was a lab with thick fur, and you could still smell it on him six months later."

"And the living room carpet?"

"My mother always wanted hardwood floors anyway," she said.

"So, did the skunk incident curb your desire to investigate things?"

"No way. It just reminded me to be careful how I go about it."

Matt focused on his food so he could keep his mind off the beautiful but disconcerting woman across the table. He had an important job to do.

A glance at the time on his cell phone told him that his crew would be arriving on-site in less than seven hours. Late nights with Caroline Bennett wouldn't further his cause, and her penchant for asking tough questions might cause him a major headache.

"Did you have a dog when you were a kid?" she asked.

"Beagle. His name was Benson."

"Benson the beagle, I like it."

"My dad loved that dog, but he—"

Matt remembered the dog barking madly when the police came to haul his dad away. His mother had leashed the dog and handed the leash to Matt. As Matt had stood on the front lawn with his mother and his little brother watching their dad get in the back seat of a police car, Benson had howled as if he were losing his own father.

When Matt and his brother had visited their dad in prison for the first time, he remembered his father asking about the dog and nearly breaking down in tears when he heard Benson had gone to an animal shelter.

Did his father shed tears over the fact that he and his brother and his mother had lived in a shelter for a week while the police treated their home as if it were a crime scene?

"I'm sorry," Caroline said. "I can see this is a sad story for you. I wish dogs would live as long as people."

Matt cleared his throat.

"I was talking to Virginia Hamilton while we worked the 5K," Caroline said. "She told me about her dog, Betty, passing away last winter. She's thinking of getting a puppy. You could get a dog."

Matt shook his head. "I work too many hours when the weather is nice, and I don't think a dog would appreciate waiting inside on sunny days."

When they finished eating, Caroline took the check from the waitress and paid the bill. They headed to the parking lot where Matt opened the passenger door of his truck for Caroline to get in. The truck noise forced their silence as they crossed the bridge, but Matt cut the engine when he pulled into the lot in front of Caroline's dorm.

"Thanks for the food and company," he said.

"You're welcome. Thanks for being my victim in the class tonight. Virginia said she'd find some extra volunteers for the other nights, so you don't have to come. Unless you want to."

Did he want to? Matt hadn't made a fool of himself over a girl in a long time. There'd been a few relationships in college, but even though one of them had lasted an entire semester, he was quite sure he hadn't felt anything like the emotional roller coaster Caroline put him on.

The smart choice would be to cut a wide swath around her.

"I'll see what my schedule looks like," Matt said.

Caroline put a hand on the door lever, but then turned to him and paused, lips slightly parted for a few seconds. Had she not been a police officer with a powerful curiosity about an incident involving his family, he might have leaned forward and kissed her.

But that was a risk he was not ready to take.

CHAPTER TWELVE

"So what happened after I left last night? Did you go on a date with the teacher?" Lucas asked.

The day after the self-defense class, Lucas and Matt were spending the evening at their parents' home in Bayside. The brick home on the lake was part of a small community of similar structures. All of them had wide front lawns and a sweeping back lawn that led down to the water. Most houses, including the Corbin house, also had a dock.

Growing up there had been like a dream for Matt and his brother. The comfort and luxury went a long way toward erasing the pain in their mother's eyes whenever their former life came up.

"I didn't go on a date with the teacher," Matt said. "And I sure hope you didn't tell Mom any of this."

"Haven't had a chance to since I got home late last night and worked all day."

"Good."

Matt handed his brother the screwdriver he was using to dismantle a dock light while they waited for dinner to be ready. The thirty-foot steel dock was only ten years old, but the wiring was temperamental.

"Can you get some caulk from the garage?" Matt asked. "I think if I seal this light fixture it won't draw moisture and go out all the time. I'm sure Dad is tired of changing the bulb."

"Be right back."

Matt sat on the dock and waited for his brother to make the quick trip across the lawn. Finding the caulk in the well-organized garage would only take moments.

The sun slanted across the bay and lit the small waves with color. Across the water, lights on the Starlight Point roller coasters contrasted with the darkening sky. The view from his rented house wedged in a downtown neighborhood was lousy by comparison, but he was twenty-six. Too old to live with his parents.

His brother was still in college and kept

his room at home for breaks and summer. Lucas had considered living in the dorms at the Point, but he'd opted for a comfortable bed and his own bathroom. The sunroom on the back of the house was also his temporary art studio. With good lighting and plenty of space, Lucas spent the hours he wasn't drawing caricatures at the Point there.

He was working on a book of illustrations as part of a joint project with an English major at his college. Matt had been surprised when Lucas had wanted to show him the work in progress when he'd first arrived for dinner.

In the past, Lucas had been very guarded about letting anyone, even his family, see his work. But his younger brother had opened up lately. Perhaps it was the experience of drawing portraits on an open midway while guests waited and cable cars traveled overhead. It was hard to have secrets in a place as wide-open and populated as Starlight Point.

Lucas came back with a tube of caulk and a dispenser. He handed it to his brother.

"So, tell me about the date you didn't go

on with the lady who was not our teacher," he said.

"We went to the Pony Express. I had a burger. She had the chicken basket."

"And?"

"And we talked."

"Did she talk about all the ways she could kill or maim you if she wanted?"

Matt laughed. "It didn't come up. I think it was already implied in the class."

He laid a neat line of caulk around the bottom of the dock light to prevent moisture from seeping up from the ground. As he replaced the top of the fixture and screwed it down, he glanced along the row of lights. There were half a dozen.

"I probably should do all of these," he said.

"I'll take them apart if you'll do the caulking," Lucas offered.

They worked together in silence for a few minutes. Matt wondered how much he should share with his brother about Caroline and her curiosity about the Loose Cannon.

"We talked about dogs," he said suddenly. "Do you remember Benson?"

"A little. Mom has a picture of us with Benson in front of the Christmas tree."

"Caroline had a dog that got sprayed by a skunk."

"Messy. And wonderful date conversation. I hope you did better than that."

Matt shrugged. "We talked about college some. And what drives us, I guess."

"I know what drives you."

The way Lucas said it made Matt wonder how obvious it was.

"What do you think drives me?" he asked as he tightened the top of the third light.

Lucas sat on the dock next to him and swung his legs. "Fear. Same thing that drives me. Fear of being like our dad. Fear of failing and being a giant disappointment to our mom. Fear of letting down Bruce, who's been like finding the gold at the end of a rainbow for our family." He lay back on the dock. "I've never said that out loud before and now I sound like I'm afraid of breathing. Pathetic."

"Not pathetic," Matt said. "But unless you're embezzling hundreds of thousands from the caricature stand on the midway, you're in no danger of being like our dad."

"I'd hate prison," Lucas said. "Can't imagine staring at white walls all day long."

"And getting outside once a day if you're lucky." Matt almost shuddered. One of the many things he loved about his construction job was being outside, even dealing with snow, mud and rain. Being the boss on the job site also represented freedom to him, something he valued as much as the good opinion of his family.

"So what's her deal?" Lucas asked.

"She loves justice."

"Doesn't everyone?"

"Not like she does. She has this burning thirst to figure out mysteries and haul guilty parties before the jury. It's a little scary."

"Only if you're hiding something, I suppose," Lucas said. He sat up, but continued swinging his feet off the dock while Matt caulked the last light. "I wonder what made her that way."

Matt wondered the same thing. He'd almost asked her directly but relented.

"She's interested in the Loose Cannon," Matt said. He lowered his voice when he said the name of the ride, even though a wide lawn separated them from the house where his mother was finalizing dinner and his stepfather was probably upstairs changing out of his work clothes.

Lucas narrowed his eyes. "What's there to find out? The ride failed, they tore it down. End of story."

"It's uncomfortable. And weird. I always assumed Uncle John sold the business to Bruce because he felt as if he'd failed. Especially when he got the contract to tear down something he'd just built. Can't imagine what that would feel like."

Lucas laughed. "You're not going to add that to your truckload of stuff to worry about, are you? Don't even think you'll end up tearing down the Shooting Star in your lifetime. Not going to happen."

"You never know what's going to happen. I'm sure Uncle John never thought he would."

"Did you ever think it was strange that Starlight Point didn't give that ride much of a chance? They tore it down after only one season. Doesn't seem like they were even trying."

Matt shoved the screwdriver in his back pocket and picked up the caulk gun. "It was a nasty accident. Killed a girl. That kind of bad publicity doesn't go away."

"So what does Sherlock Holmes think she's going to find out about it?"

Matt looked across the darkening water at Starlight Point. Next year, a giant new coaster would tower over the skyline and mingle with the existing ones. He hoped it would never be dogged with an accident like the Loose Cannon. If he did something wrong as he built it, could someone die? How would he live with that guilt?

Had Uncle John done something wrong? Matt didn't even want to consider it. He swallowed the thought like a bitter pill. "I don't know what Caroline thinks she'll find. And even though there was obviously nothing criminal that went on, her questions make me uncomfortable. It seems as if she suspects something, but I don't know why."

"Is it about that other guy who was killed around the same time? The maintenance guy?"

Matt nodded. "I think that's part of it."

"Well," Lucas said as he got to his feet, "she sure can't blame that part on Uncle John's construction company."

"No." Matt rolled his shoulders. "I just don't like having it all brought up. It's like having a stranger dig around in your attic and judge your family. We don't need any hint of bad publicity, and Bruce doesn't need one more thing to weigh on his bad heart."

"Dinner," their mother called from the patio door.

Matt and Lucas headed for the garage to stow their tools before sitting down at the table. As they crossed the lawn, Matt wondered if his brother was right. There was nothing to those old stories, and they couldn't hurt Bayside Construction now, no matter how hard Caroline looked in old dusty corners.

CHAPTER THIRTEEN

IN ONE OF her criminal justice classes, Caroline's professor had made an important point about the value of listening. Their class had taken several field trips and each student was required to write down everything they heard. They'd gone outside where the distant noise of trains mingled with birdcalls, wind and car traffic. At a local coffee shop, students hunched over their drinks listening to conversations at nearby tables. They'd even gone to a baseball game on campus and a bank during busy Friday hours.

Caroline had been amazed by the different sounds and impressions the students had heard. How could two people sitting side by side at a coffee shop come away with different perspectives on a neighboring table's conversation? This summer, wherever she was posted at Starlight Point, Caroline had resolved to practice listening.

Most days, it was a failure. The scrambler ride created a whooshing wind noise. The roller coaster down the midway clacked and induced screaming. Lots of screaming. The train whistled and puffed. Kids cried and yelled. Sometimes parents cried and yelled, depending on how their day was going.

Starlight Point was a cacophony of noise. Which was one of the reasons Caroline was happy to take an early morning shift even though it would be a long day with another STRIPE class scheduled for the evening.

Beginning in the cool morning air at seven o'clock, Caroline gradually added sounds to her collection. Employees arriving, vehicles on the Outer Loop road, rides groaning into action for their first guests. Eventually it would become deafening, but the rise in volume was gradual over the first several hours of her shift.

At around nine in the morning, Caroline heard the park coming to life. But she could still hear the construction sounds from behind the fence. Those noises of trucks, backup alarms, digging and men shouting over their own noise had become her early morning friends, a constant assurance that work was progressing.

But something was not right. She heard beeping that indicated reverse gear on some large piece of equipment, but when it stopped she heard something else. Shouting. Voices raised not in anger or greeting or directions, but fear and panic instead.

"Get it off him. Off. Hurry!"

A door slammed. More shouting, and the voices held wild notes of panic.

Something was definitely wrong. It was not her job to open the gate and snoop on the construction zone, but she didn't need her police training to know those shouts were fueled by something bad.

Caroline unlocked the gate closest to the midway and swung it open. The usual trucks, steel beams, piles of earth and stone, and excavating equipment littered the site.

But all the men were grouped around the back of one of the dump trucks. At least one person was on the ground. Her heart raced as she looked for Matt in the chaos. She found him.

He stood over the man on the ground, one hand over his eyes and holding his cell phone to his ear. Although his posture suggested he was in agony, he appeared physically unharmed. Caroline's relief at finding Matt on his feet was so strong she wondered how much room she'd allowed him in her heart. And how much more she should.

Caroline dashed across the uneven ground, hoping she could help. She'd completed first responder and CPR training in college. Without hesitation or fear, she parted the circle of men standing around their coworker on the ground. She noticed their faces. Wide eyes, mouths open, even a few tears. Her eyes dropped to the man on the ground. Was he dead?

A man kneeling next to the injured worker was talking to him, and Caroline noticed a small movement in response. His chest rose and lowered with breath. Not dead, thank goodness. But what had happened?

Matt finished his call and slid his phone into his pocket.

"What can I do?" Caroline asked. She'd heard him give an exact location over the phone. Any 911 calls from Starlight Point were directed to the dispatcher at the Starlight Point police station, so an ambulance was only moments away.

He shook his head, his jaw tight. She watched him swallow hard as if he were trying to force down terrible emotions.

"Guide the ambulance when it gets here."

"I'll get the gate on the Outer Loop open and wait there," she said. How she wished she could erase the pain on his face. "What happened?"

"Run over by that truck. His legs…"

Caroline's need to ask questions and seek answers nearly clawed its way to the front line of the conversation. She wanted to ask how it happened, who was driving the truck and how many witnesses there were. She *would* ask those questions. Later. She'd have to for the report.

The man on the ground was still, his skin growing even paler. Tension radiated from the circle of workers. They looked to Matt as if he held the answers, even though there was nothing anyone could do until the ambulance arrived. Caroline abandoned the questions she desperately wanted to ask and headed for the gate.

She pulled the radio off her belt and informed the dispatcher she'd have the Outer Loop gate open and reiterated which gate it was. The fire and ambulance crew used the same frequency the police did, and she knew they'd hear her message. She wanted to add a special request that they hurry, but she knew they always did.

Matt was competent and trustworthy. Of course he'd already conveyed the extent and seriousness of the worker's injuries when he called it in.

Waiting, even though it was only minutes before she heard the siren approaching, was torture. She looked back at the construction site. Matt was on his phone again, and the other men stood over their coworker, shoulders slumped. One of them still knelt next to the injured man, talking to him. What had happened?

At last. The ambulance slowed and Caroline positioned herself in the driver's view of his side mirror so she could give him hand signals as he backed in. Every minute counted.

As soon as the ambulance stopped, her brother jumped out of the passenger side door. The chief of the Starlight Point Fire

Department, he still responded to emergency calls, especially ones that were serious.

She was relieved to see him because, even though he'd tortured her as a child by hiding frogs in her bedroom and stealing her french fries, he was the most dependable person she knew. If the injured man's life and legs could be saved, Scott would make sure it happened.

Scott nodded at her, but his expression was all business. He and his partner jerked the gurney out of the back of the ambulance and placed it next to the injured man. Scott knelt and assessed the situation, talking to the patient and giving directions to his partner and the other men standing around. Caroline waited, radio in hand, in case her brother needed her to call for backup.

Matt knelt next to Scott, obviously offering to help. Caroline watched him hold a splint by the man's injured legs while Scott and his partner secured it. He looked up at her once and their eyes connected. Even that brief contact showed her the pain Matt was in. She wanted to help, but as a police officer, not a paramedic, it was her responsibility to secure the scene.

The backup ambulance arrived and two more paramedics immediately began assisting with the patient. Matt got up and stood next to Caroline, watching the scene on the ground unfold.

"Are you okay?" she asked him.

"No. But I'm better than he is."

"You're not injured, are you?" she asked. Caroline felt off-balance, nervous, because she didn't have the facts of the accident. How had it happened? Who was involved?

Matt shook his head. "Jackson is one of my best guys. Worked with him on several projects, heck of a nice guy."

"Do you know what happened?"

"Truck backed over him. Crushed his legs. I didn't see it, but I heard the yelling."

"Did anyone witness it?"

Matt cut her a look. "We can do the report later, and you can interrogate the rest of the guys then."

Caroline sucked in a sharp breath at his tone. "That's not what I meant."

Matt passed a hand over his eyes. "Sorry."

They watched the paramedics working

under the careful direction of Caroline's brother. They secured Jackson to a backboard, immobilizing him before lifting him onto the gurney. Instead of rolling it, four men lifted the cot and slid it carefully into the ambulance.

"I called his wife," Matt told Scott. "She'll meet you at the hospital in Bayside."

Scott nodded, a grim expression on his face. "They're probably going to transfer him right away to a trauma hospital, but she'll get to see him before he goes."

Caroline's brother was always serious about his job and safety. But his face carried the ultra-serious expression he only reserved for especially somber events. She'd seen it on several occasions, especially last summer when Scott pulled Evie Hamilton out of a burning hotel, saving her life.

"Will he be okay?" she asked her brother softly.

Scott wrinkled his brow. "His legs are bad. Could have internal bleeding. Lucky the ground was fairly soft so there was a little give. He's looking at surgery and a very long recovery."

Caroline's brother got in the driver's seat, activated the flashing lights and drove carefully out of the construction zone. She heard him turn on the siren a moment later as he skirted the parking lot and headed for the Point Bridge.

"Anything I can do?" she asked Matt. She'd asked once before and already knew the answer, but she wanted to reach out to him and try to erase the heartache he obviously felt for his employee.

Matt's phone rang and took his attention away from her. As he held the phone in his hand and read the screen for the caller's identity, Caroline noticed his hand shaking.

"My brother," he told Caroline as he swiped to answer the phone.

Giving Matt privacy to talk to Lucas, Caroline joined the group of men talking with the police chief and another officer. The construction workers stared at the ground and occasionally cast nervous glances at each other.

There would be tough questions to ask for the official report, and it appeared the police chief had already started.

"I'M DRIVING INTO the parking lot when I see an ambulance go flying out of your construction zone," Lucas said. "You better not be in it."

"One of my guys," Matt explained, his hand gripping his cell phone. "Truck backed over him."

"Is he okay?"

"No. His legs were crushed, and I don't know what else. All I know is he's still alive. Thank God."

"Don't those trucks have backup alarms?" Lucas asked.

"Yes, but if you hang around construction sites long enough, you start to hear those alarms in your sleep."

"Did you talk to Bruce yet and tell him what's going on?"

"No," Matt said. The last thing he wanted to do was pile more worry on his stepfather, especially with his heart condition. But Bruce was his next phone call. He owned the business, and he had to be informed, especially with a case of a serious employee injury. Matt's heart was heavy, hoping his friend and employee Jackson would be all right. It was also heavy with doubt.

Whenever something bad happened on a construction job, the man in charge was responsible. Could Matt have done something to prevent it? Jackson might never walk again, work again. How could Matt live with knowing the accident happened on his watch?

Bruce had every right to wonder if leaving the construction business to Matt was a smart move. Matt wondered about it himself.

"I'm headed to the hospital in a few minutes," he told his brother. "I'll call you later."

Matt's boots felt as if they were filled with concrete as he trudged back to the circle of his workers. A tight-knit crew, they had built a gymnasium for the Catholic school in town and a warehouse for a local manufacturing company over the winter. Earlier in the spring, they'd finished an outdoor recreation area complete with ropes courses and water slides for a local hotel that wanted to offer its guests a resort experience.

And those projects were only part of their schedule for the past year. The coaster was the largest project they'd tackled as a team, but it was also the largest project the Bayside area had seen in years.

He knew his men were hurting. Especially the man who was driving the truck, whoever that was. Assigning blame had been the last thing on his mind while Jackson lay on the ground drifting in and out of consciousness. Now that there was nothing he could do to help his injured employee, Matt stopped and listened to the questions from the police chief.

Caroline stood next to her boss, writing down statements and filling out what was probably an official report on a clipboard. *Paperwork.* He'd known it was coming.

"And you say you didn't see him behind the truck," Chief Walker said.

"I did see him," Babcock said. "At first. He was helping me back between two posts we already set. I saw him in my side mirror and then he was gone."

Will Babcock was old enough to be Matt's father, and he'd been with Bayside Construction as long as Matt could remember. He was no-nonsense and efficient, even with a bad back resulting from years of heavy manual labor.

"Where did you think he went?" Caroline asked. "When you didn't see him in your mirror any longer?"

Matt stiffened at her tone. There was a

hint of accusation in it. He had to admit he was wondering the same thing, but life in a construction zone was never neat and tidy. Distractions and hazards were lurking everywhere. Did Caroline realize that?

"It's a construction zone," Babcock said. "I sure as hell didn't think he went out for ice cream."

"Easy, Babcock," Matt said. "It's just a question." And cooperating was going to make this a lot easier, he thought.

"You think I'd run over him if I saw him back there? We've been friends for years. I went to his wedding."

"I know," Matt said. "We're all friends." Babcock's initial stunned silence after the accident had turned into anger. His face was red and his voice shook. Emotions were high, but it was Matt's job to show leadership, no matter how uncertain he felt right now.

"So, he disappeared from your view in the side mirror and you kept backing up," the police chief said, keeping his tone even. "What happened next?"

"That's when I heard the screaming."

"Who was screaming?" Caroline asked.

"I was," Walton said. Walton was the member of their crew with the most explosive temper. Matt had seen him throw a hammer in frustration, kick the heck out of a truck tire and lay out a string of expletives when things weren't going his way. At the moment, however, he was icy calm.

"I didn't see how it happened, but I turned around from what I was doing and saw the truck go right—" he paused and his jaw worked "—right over Jackson. And then stop. That's why I was yelling. The truck was on him."

Caroline was listening and nodding. She must have been right outside the gate and she probably heard the same words that had caught Matt's attention. A desperate shout telling the truck driver to get the truck off the injured man. If he lived a hundred years, Matt would never forget hearing Walton's yell.

The police chief sent an assessing look around the group. "Anyone witness it? See exactly how it happened?"

The other six men shook their heads. They'd been doing their jobs, same as Matt.

He hadn't seen it either, and he shook his head along with his crew.

The chief inspected the back of the truck, looking carefully at the tires. "For your own benefit, I want you to turn this truck on and put it in reverse. I need to hear that the alarm is functional so I can include it in the report," the chief said.

No one volunteered. No one wanted to touch the truck that had just nearly killed and probably crippled their friend and co-worker.

"I'll do it," Matt said.

He climbed into the driver's seat, turned the key and put the truck in reverse. He kept his foot firmly on the brakes, not wanting a repeat of the morning's tragedy. Everyone, including Matt, heard the familiar beeping of the backup alarm. Matt let it beep for a few seconds longer to assure the police chief there was no mechanical failure to blame, and then he took the truck out of gear and turned it off. He didn't want to get out of the driver's seat. He sat there for a moment, wishing he could start the day over.

It only took a fraction of a second to change someone's life. How he wished he could give Jackson back those seconds so he wouldn't be in an ambulance right now.

Matt pulled himself together and climbed out of the truck, knowing his crew needed him now more than ever. When he went around the truck, the chief and Caroline were both squatting and peering under the axle. Caroline was pointing at something and talking in low tones to her boss.

Matt's heart sank. What did they see? Had he failed to maintain the truck? Was he to blame for the workplace accident?

His worst nightmare. Letting down Bruce Corbin. Letting down his crew. Letting down the company he'd hoped to inherit in order to secure a future for his mother and brother.

Matt glanced at his crew. Their shattered faces and silence spoke for them. Like him, they all knew the accident could just as easily have happened to any of them. It was the life of a construction crew, working daily with dangerous equipment, timelines, weather and land conditions that were sometimes beyond their control.

"That could be it," Caroline said.

Matt poked his head under the back of

the truck, ready to face whatever the police had found.

Caroline was pointing at a bar of rolled steel. About three inches in diameter and six feet long, it sat under the truck. There were dozens of pieces just like it scattered around the construction zone. Sometimes used in reinforcing concrete, sometimes as part of the framing structure.

"What could be it?" he asked. What did the steel have to do with the accident?

"Maybe he tripped over that and fell. That's why the driver didn't see him," Caroline said. "Or he might have stepped on it and it rolled out from under his foot."

It was plausible. But what did it matter? Matt knew it was an accident, no matter how it happened. And finding a piece of steel to blame didn't change the fact that one of his men was severely injured and the rest of them felt as if they'd been punched. Especially the driver of the truck.

"Could be," Matt acknowledged without much enthusiasm.

Caroline looked strangely excited about her discovery. Her cheeks were flushed and she spoke rapidly. "I'll bet that's what happened," she said.

Matt was in no mood to enjoy resolving mysteries or solving riddles. It wouldn't help Jackson right now—he was probably arriving at the hospital at the same time as his panicked wife.

Matt remembered meeting Jackson's wife at their wedding and at the company Christmas party. She was in her midtwenties like her husband. Too young to be facing today's disaster.

"Chief," Matt said, "do you see a problem with me leaving right now? I want to go to the hospital and talk to Jackson's wife. I have to make a few calls first so I can assure her we'll do everything we can to get him back on his feet."

The chief nodded. "Just don't take this truck. Otherwise, you're all free to go. This isn't a crime scene."

Without looking at Caroline, Matt turned and addressed his crew. "Button up the site as best you can and go home for the day. I'll send text updates on Jackson. We'll meet at the office tomorrow morning at six and talk about this." He lowered his voice and glanced around the group. "Take care of yourselves, guys."

He put a hand on Babcock's shoulder as he passed him, hoping the gesture would convey what words could not. As he walked to his truck parked near the fence, Matt heard footsteps behind him. He stopped and turned.

It was Caroline, but her expression was no longer that of an archeologist discovering a long-forgotten cache of treasure.

"I don't want to talk about it, Caroline," he said.

"Okay."

She fell into step beside him as they picked their way across the uneven ground. "I just wanted to catch up with you to say I'm sorry this happened and offer to help if I can."

"You aren't hunting for more clues?" he asked.

She drew a quick breath and he berated himself for his lousy tone. He was surprised she continued to walk with him to his truck. If someone talked to him like that, he'd head the other way.

When they got to his truck, Caroline leaned

on the driver's door and crossed her arms over her chest.

"Sorry about saying that," Matt said.

"People say all kinds of things when they're upset. It's been a terrible morning, a huge shock."

Matt took off his hard hat and rolled his head back. The sky was bright blue. It would be a beautiful day, but Jackson wouldn't see any of it.

"It's shocking, but it isn't. Accidents happen all the time in work zones. It's a dangerous job." He met her eyes and waited a beat. "Accidents," he repeated.

Caroline bit her lip and drew her eyebrows together. "I always want to find out exactly what happened and why. Maybe it's my police training. I'm afraid if I shrug and call something an accident, it belittles it. It means I'm not searching for answers anymore. And people deserve answers. Always."

Matt waited. There were many things he didn't know about her, but he could see she was having a hard time accepting this for what it was.

"Some things just…happen," Matt said.

His words felt empty, but he didn't know what to say.

Instead of answering him, Caroline shoved off from the door of his truck and gave him a quick, hard hug. He barely had time to register the feeling of her arms around his chest and her hair tickling his chin. The hug was over in just seconds, but he didn't think he'd soon forget it. She was softer than he'd imagined. *Had he imagined how she'd feel?* And she smelled like she looked. Feminine, but without fuss.

What on earth made her hug him like that?

Caroline released him and lingered, her face only inches from his.

Matt had never doubted his own strength, both physical and emotional. But somehow he felt stronger because of her. He realized how nice it would be to have her by his side, but then he remembered his problems were his own—to shoulder and resolve. There were no easy answers for him, no downtime.

Perhaps Caroline saw the reserve in his expression because she lightly patted his shoulder and walked away.

As Matt turned to watch her leave, still

mystified by her actions, he saw the police chief staring at them. Would Caroline be in trouble for hugging a contractor while officially on duty? Matt doubted it.

But he was sure of one thing. The police chief looked just as confused as Matt felt, and the day was far from over for both of them.

CHAPTER FOURTEEN

"I'M SORRY," Caroline told a little girl at the ride entrance. "The Scrambler is closed for maintenance right now."

"How long?"

"I wish I could tell you, but I don't know. Maybe you could stop by later?"

The girl and her mother wore matching purple T-shirts, a wise move for keeping track of each other in the crowd. It was a Wednesday afternoon in mid-July, the height of the tourist season. It was also Caroline's twenty-first birthday, but she didn't mind being at work. Her parents were coming all the way from their new home in Arizona on the weekend and taking her out to a nice dinner with her brother and Evie.

As she watched the little girl and her mother walk away hand in hand, Caroline smiled, remembering the year she and her mother wore matching dresses for Easter.

Mel Preston whacked a bolt into place on one of the mechanical arms of the ride. The head of maintenance, he was married to June Hamilton, which technically made him an in-law. She leaned over the fence surrounding the ride and spoke just loudly enough over the general cacophony of Starlight Point for him to hear her.

"Think you can fix it?"

"Trying," Mel said. He used the sleeve of his blue uniform shirt to wipe sweat from his brow. The midday sun was brutal as it bounced off the white concrete.

"Can I help?"

"Toss me a bolt from that bag."

Caroline shoved her hand into a heavy bag filled with bolts and pulled several out. "Does it matter which one?"

"Need a grade eight," he said. He sat back on his haunches while he waited for her to sort out the right bolt. "Lot of pressure and tension on this beam."

"So one marked five won't work?"

"It might work for a while, but I wouldn't trust it for this."

The grade five bolt in George Dupont's pocket tormented her. Did that bolt come from the Loose Cannon? If so, why had he picked it up? Did it have anything to do with how he died?

Someone tapped Caroline on the shoulder and she whirled around. It was a teenager holding a large green alligator he'd probably won from one of the game booths.

"Is this ride going to open today?" the boy asked. He leaned to the side and looked around Caroline just as they both heard a loud clanking sound followed by Mel saying, "Dangit."

"I picked a lousy day to come here," the kid muttered as he slouched off.

"You've worked here a long time, haven't you?" Caroline asked, turning back to Mel.

"Thirteen years."

"Are there some guys who've been here even longer?"

Caroline wanted to ask specifically who might have been here in the summer of 1985, but she doubted Mel would know that and she didn't want to have to explain her reason for asking.

"Sure."

"They must feel a lot of loyalty to Starlight Point," she said.

"We all do," Mel said. He glanced up from his job, hammer in hand. "Don't we?"

"Of course," Caroline answered quickly. And she did. But if she had to make a choice between protecting Starlight Point or revealing evidence, she knew what she would do. Justice was more important than business.

Was it more important than family and relationships? She considered the question as she watched people walk by. An older couple moved slowly past. A teenaged couple with their arms around each other's waists. A family with two little boys wearing red T-shirts with construction trucks on them.

The maintenance man who died was someone's son. And the girl who was thrown from the Loose Cannon was someone's daughter—her neighbors'—and they'd never had the closure and justice they deserved.

Several hours later, Caroline clocked out and headed for the post office in downtown Bayside. Her parents were coming in a few days, but she knew her mother would also mail a card—something pretty with a nice verse about her birthday. Her mother also tended to underline phrases she thought particularly appropriate; it was her way to personalize standard greeting cards from the store.

But along with the purple envelope sparkling with glitter stuffed into her mailbox was a large brown envelope with a return address of the offices of the State of Michigan.

It had been over six weeks, and Caroline had nearly given up on getting copies of the official report from the agency that inspected amusement park rides back in the 1980s. The department of commerce had converted to computers sometime in the past three decades, but the documents she wanted predated the modernization. It had been a long wait.

"Happy birthday to me," she said to herself. Back at her dorm, she climbed the stairs to her room, two at a time, eager to change her clothes and settle in to read the lengthy report. Perhaps it would contain the answers she'd been waiting for. Would there be details about the construction of the ride? Maybe a clue about the grade of the bolts used or an explanation why the murdered man had a broken grade five bolt in his pocket?

When she got to the third floor of her dorm, she both heard and felt loud music coming from the room across the hall. The three boys who lived there worked nights emptying the dumpsters and cleaning the restrooms, and they usually slept all morning. It was a lousy job, and she couldn't blame them for wanting to enjoy their afternoons and evenings.

However, their speakers shook the floor and rattled her ears. There was no way she could read a detailed report with that racket. She let herself into her room, changed into shorts and a T-shirt, and opened the birthday card from her mother.

There were butterflies and flowers in watercolor with a lengthy poem about the blessings of daughters. Her mother had underlined the words *loving*, *beautiful*, *smart* and *joy*. If her mother knew how close Caroline was to marching down the hallway and letting the person playing that loud music know how she felt, she might've chosen some different adjectives.

Instead of picking a fight with the night-shift boys, Caroline headed outside. The July day was still hot, but she knew of a picnic table near the marina where a shade tree combined with the lake breeze would provide all the comfort she needed as she settled in to read.

Envelope under her arm, she practically trotted to the picnic table and was delighted to find it empty. She wished she'd remembered a drink or a snack, but it would have to wait. Caroline slid her finger under the flap of the envelope and opened it. The weight of the package told her there were dozens of pages inside.

Dozens. Typed on a typewriter. Plus pictures and some handwritten notes. This would take hours to read. It was like a time capsule of record-keeping from another age. The pictures and pages were photocopied, so the quality was a disappointment. But Caroline still had hope the reports would be a revelation—if the inspector had done his job. She wondered if the reports she wrote this summer would ever be read with anticipation in the future.

The first page was a cover page, nothing

but details about the contents of the file and location of the reports from the office in the state capital. Caroline shuffled that page to the bottom of the stack and prepared to read. The next page was a narrative, entirely filled with typed text.

"Are you spending your birthday doing paperwork?"

Caroline jumped at the voice behind her and swung around, the papers clutched tight in one hand.

"Easy," Matt said, both hands up. "I should probably know better than to sneak up on a police officer."

"You shouldn't be able to sneak up on a police officer," Caroline said. Her pulse beat in her throat.

Matt jerked his head toward the amusement park entrance. "All that noise covered my footsteps." He walked around the picnic table where he could face her and swung one leg over the bench. He'd clearly just come from the construction site. He wore a button-down cotton shirt, jeans and work boots.

Caroline shoved the papers back into the brown envelope and laid it face down on the table. Matt's eyes dipped to the envelope and returned to her face.

"Top secret?" he asked.

"Just something I'm studying. How is Jackson?"

"Better. He only needed surgery on one leg, and there were no internal injuries."

"He was lucky," Caroline said quietly.

"Like your brother said, the ground was soft so when the truck went over him…well, it could've been worse."

"Do you think he'll be able to come back to work?"

He nodded. "We hope. But it'll be a while."

"And how is the man who was driving the truck?"

"Babcock," Matt said. "He's pretty shaken up. He went over to Jackson's house and mowed the lawn. He's also taking care of Jackson's dog while he's in the hospital because his wife's there with him all the time."

"That's a nice gesture."

"I think it makes him feel better to help out. Accidents on construction sites happen, and they're almost as bad for the person who causes it as the guy who's the victim. It's something we talk about a lot. We have mandatory safety training, but nothing reminds you of how fast something can happen like an actual accident."

Matt laid both forearms on the table and leaned toward her. Caroline noticed dust in his hair. His eyes were green. Kind. He truly cared about the men who worked for him. Cared about doing the job right. Were all construction companies run like his? Was his uncle's?

Too bad all men weren't like him. Conscientious, hardworking, tall and muscular, ready with a quick smile.

What was she thinking?

She'd had a serious plan for the summer when she'd arrived at Starlight Point, and it didn't include romance. But if she were going to have a summer romance...

"I have a problem," Matt said, interrupting her thoughts.

"A legal problem?" she asked, a little breathlessly. She hoped her thoughts didn't show on her face. "Something missing from your site or vehicle damage or...something?"

"I'm hungry."

"Oh."

"And I hoped you'd help me out."

"I'm not hiding a picnic basket under this table," Caroline said.

"Do you have dinner plans?"

Caroline hadn't made plans for dinner. And if she had she would've cancelled them when she discovered the state report in her mail. Her fingers drummed lightly on the envelope as she considered her answer. She decided to go with the truth.

"No," she admitted. "My brother is working overtime, and my parents aren't coming until the weekend."

"I hate to see you eating alone."

"Because it's my birthday?"

"That's not the only reason," he said. He leaned closer and Caroline wasn't sure if she should lean away or toward him. She felt her lips curve in a smile at the irresistible man in front of her.

"Have dinner with me. Please," he said. "If you don't want to get in my loud truck—which is a mess right now anyway—we can eat right here at the marina restaurant."

Caroline hesitated, her fingers flipping the corner of the envelope. She'd waited six weeks. Another hour or two seemed unbearable. But then again, she'd already waited six weeks. What would a few more hours matter?

"You're not planning to tell the wait staff it's my birthday, are you? I hate it when they gather around the table clapping and singing."

"I promise I won't," he said, laughing. "I always feel sorry for the waiters when that happens. They can't enjoy it, and it probably just puts them behind on their work."

Why does he have to be so perfect?

"Then I'd love to have dinner with you."

"Great. Thanks."

She picked up her envelope and stood. Should she take it back to her dorm or just tuck it under her arm as if it weren't terribly important?

"I hope we don't have to wait for a table," Matt commented as he untangled his long legs from the picnic table. "I'm starving."

Well, that settled it. She turned away from the dorms and walked alongside Matt across the parking lot to the marina restaurant. Part of a major renovation the previous summer, the marina restaurant and docks still looked new. It was nearly six o'clock, and the sky was still bright. Beautiful boats were tied up in long rows.

As they approached the entrance to the restaurant, Caroline was happy to find there was no line snaking out the front door. A good sign. Matt held the door for her and they entered the cool restaurant.

He put a hand on her back as they followed the waitress to a table by the windows. Despite the air-conditioned blast on her skin, Caroline knew it was Matt's touch that brought out goose bumps on her arms. Although she'd taken him down in self-defense class and then given him an impulsive hug just yesterday, it was the first time he'd touched her as if they were a couple, and something about it felt very right.

"Do you have a birthday tradition at your house?" Matt asked after he'd decided a well-done steak would be worth the wait and Caroline had echoed his order. With a side of fries and a plate of appetizers on the way, he imagined he'd survive. His stomach was one concern. The beautiful woman across the table from him was another.

Caroline shrugged and smiled. "I usually

have dinner with strangers I lure in by looking lonely."

"That sounds dangerous."

Caroline raised an eyebrow.

"Okay, maybe not for someone with your skills." He sipped his iced tea and enjoyed the cool liquid going down his hot, dusty throat. "And I'm not a stranger," Matt said.

Caroline's smile faded and Matt felt as if he were a museum object being scrutinized by a graduate student. Would she get out her notebook or fingerprint kit? When Caroline tucked her hair behind her ears and her smile returned, Matt felt as if he'd been chosen for a special collection.

"No, you're not a stranger. I know quite a lot about you."

And did she like what she knew? More important, how would she feel about the things she didn't know?

"Give me the list while we wait. It'll take my mind off my stomach."

Caroline counted off each fact using the fingers of her left hand as if she were doing math problems in the air. "I know where you work, what you drive and what you usually wear. I've seen this shirt," she said, pointing at his favorite but threadbare blue button-down, "at least three times this summer."

"Is that bad?"

"No," she said. "It's a good sign. It proves you know how to do laundry. Or you're hiding a wife or girlfriend at home who does it for you."

Matt laughed. "No wife. No girlfriend."

"I didn't think so. She would probably have thrown that shirt in the trash."

Matt glanced down. Was it really so bad? "Go on with your list. I'm not sure if I should feel flattered or judged right now."

"I know your brother, and I've met your stepfather. You appear to have their trust, but more important, the Hamilton family seems to put a lot of faith in you."

"Is that a big deal?"

"Not really. They seem to like my brother, too, and he's far from perfect."

"I can assure you I'm far from perfect."

Caroline picked up her soda. Matt had considered insisting on buying her a drink for her twenty-first birthday, but he didn't question her choice.

"Tell me something imperfect about yourself," she said.

Where do I start? "Do you have all night?"

"I'm serious," Caroline said. "People who seem too perfect are usually hiding something. What are you hiding?"

Matt felt the blood drain from his face and pool in his empty belly. He considered making light of her question and joking his way past it, but he doubted his ability to fool Caroline. And she deserved better.

"I am hiding something," he said.

Caroline's eyes shifted to the envelope on the seat next to her. What was she so intent on reading that she hadn't even noticed him walking up behind her a few minutes ago? Did it have anything to do with her investigation of the Loose Cannon? All summer long, he'd been flirting with the line between friend or foe when it came to Caroline, and that line had become so blurry he no longer knew what to do about it. Except tell the truth.

"My father is a criminal."

Caroline's eyes widened, but she looked more interested than surprised.

"He's serving a long prison sentence for embezzlement."

A plate of appetizers arrived and the waitress set down smaller plates and a stack of napkins. Matt and Caroline each helped themselves to boneless wings, onion rings and potato skins.

"I used to visit him sometimes," Matt said. "But I haven't in a while. Maybe that makes me a bad son."

Caroline's mouth was open as if she was formulating a list of questions she wanted to ask. Matt steeled himself for the interrogation. It was his own fault for bringing it up.

"Did your mother and your brother go to visit him, too?"

That was what she wanted to know? It was strangely personal, far less businesslike than he might have expected.

Matt remembered the first time they'd gone as a family, and heat rolled up his neck and face. It had been humiliating, waiting with other families visiting a loved one in prison. He remembered sitting there and thinking he wasn't like them. They were tainted, somehow, by having a criminal in the family. And then he'd seen his own father—the man who'd taught him to ride a bike and who'd cut down the family Christmas tree every year— in prison orange.

And he realized he wasn't any better than the other sad and desperate families. Matt had gone back on his own several times. Once when he'd first gotten a driver's license. Again when he'd graduated from high school. And a third time when he'd finished his master's degree.

Each time he passed one of life's milestones, he tried to share it with his father. And each time it had been a bitter reminder that his father's life was an endless stream of days that were exactly the same. There were no milestones for him, only long days creeping closer to the end of his sentence.

Despite the misery of visiting his father in jail, Matt couldn't face going with his mother and his brother. It was better to face it alone and shoulder that burden for them. As far as he knew, his mother had not been to see her ex-husband in more than a decade.

The food in front of him no longer tempted him. Matt wiped his hands on his napkin and remembered he hadn't answered Caroline's question.

"Once," he said. "One time we all went together." He tried to force a smile. "It's not the world's best family activity. I was twelve that time, but my brother was only seven."

"So young to face something like that," she said. "And your mother remarried a few years later?"

He nodded. His mother had done a lot better the second time around.

"So your father is doing time for embezzlement," Caroline said matter-of-factly. "Are you a criminal, too?"

Matt felt as if he'd been slapped in the face. Until Caroline laughed and reached across the table to squeeze his hand. Her hand was smooth and much smaller than his, but its warmth erased the sting of her question.

"Judging from your reaction, I'd say the answer is no," Caroline said. "In which case, you have failed to answer my question."

"What do you mean?"

"I asked what you were hiding. Your father's crimes are his, not yours. So I still don't know what makes you less than perfect."

Matt drew a deep breath and wondered why he tortured himself by spending time with Caroline. If he could resist her, he would. Was he brave enough to reveal the one thing that tortured him and made him wonder when, not if, he would fall short? He ate an onion ring and two wings while he considered his answer.

"I pull off my clothes and throw them in the washer while they're still inside out."

She shook her head. "So? You'll have to do better than that."

"I have a birdfeeder in my yard, but I have never once put food in it. Not even last winter when the snow piled up to the bottom of the feeder."

"How do you live with yourself?" Caroline asked, smiling.

"I cut the tags off everything. Pillows, mattresses, blankets, you name it. I'm reckless about the warnings."

"Still no good. I want to know the bad thing that keeps you awake at night."

Matt leaned back and rested his shoulder blades against the hard slats of the chair.

"I'm selfish."

Caroline laughed. "You're going to have to provide evidence if you think I'm going to believe that. I've seen you bring doughnuts to your workers."

"Maybe I just want to bribe them to work faster."

"And you brought me maple-frosted ones."

"I could be buying your security skills," he said.

"Starlight Point signs my paychecks." Caroline steepled her hands, put her chin on them and stared him down. "What makes you selfish?"

Matt considered how far he wanted to go with his confession. How long had it been since he'd shared his thoughts and fears with anyone except for his brother? Something about Caroline made him want to reveal his feelings. She had a tough-cop outer shell, but he believed there was something softer on the inside.

"It would probably be in the best interest of my family if I encouraged my stepfather to sell the construction business," Matt admitted.

She wrinkled her brow, and Matt realized he'd managed to surprise her.

"You have to back up and explain. Why would he want to sell a thriving business?"

"Because," Matt said. He paused and swallowed. "He has serious health problems. Although he's just sixty-five, he has a bad heart."

Caroline gave a slight nod as if she'd already suspected Bruce's condition.

"You saw him at the media boat trip," Matt said. "And that was a good day. The doctors have told him to take it easy because there's not a lot of time left."

"So you think selling the business will allow him to retire and rest?"

"Yes. It will also provide a big payout for my mother to invest and live comfortably when Bruce is gone. She deserves that."

"Back to the selfish part," Caroline said, waving her fork for emphasis. "Tell me why you're the bad guy here."

"Because I don't want him to sell it. I want to inherit it and continue the family tradition."

Caroline didn't say anything and it made Matt want to fill the silence.

"The good family tradition of building things. Not the bad one of embezzling."

"I figured that out," Caroline said. "So, you're asking your stepfather to take a chance on you by leaving you his business instead of just selling it outright."

Matt nodded.

"If you do well, it's a happy ending for you and your mother."

"And my brother. He's got several years left in college."

"And you want to pay for that."

"Bayside Construction paid for my master's degree."

"So you think you owe everyone."

"I do."

Their food arrived, a welcome intrusion into a conversation that was starting to churn the acid in Matt's empty stomach. The steaming plates were loaded with steak, fries and asparagus spears.

"I'll never eat all this," Caroline said after the waitress left. She picked up her knife and fork. "But I'm prepared to try."

Matt chuckled. "That's what I like about you. I doubt you've ever backed down from a challenge."

"Sure I have. My mother enrolled me in dance class when I was five. She stopped taking me after a few painful weeks."

"So she was the one who gave up, not you."

"Nice try, but that was my fault. I also failed at the summer reading program at the library in sixth grade. I thought we'd be reading books, but it was glorified craft and social hour. I usually skipped the activity of the week and read mystery novels instead."

"Why am I not surprised?"

"I read an entire series of mystery books in a big blue chair by the window of the library. That was a great summer. But I never completed one single art project using macaroni and yarn."

Matt sliced off a piece of steak and chewed it slowly while he listened to Caroline describe her favorite fictional detective—a girl—who always stayed on the scent and tracked down the answer. Her eyes were bright and she talked with her hands as she relived some of the books. Matt found himself thinking how nice it would be to have dinner with her every night.

"Did that inspire you to become a police officer?" he asked. "Reading all those mystery novels?"

"No," Caroline said. "But it was part of it."

"What was the other part?"

Instead of answering, Caroline cut her steak into neat strips, then cut across the strips to make small cubes. She took her time carving up the entire piece of meat.

"It's a long story," she said.

"I'm willing to take my time eating and then order dessert. We have to have a slice of cake—even if I don't tell anyone it's a milestone birthday for you."

THIS IS OUR *second time eating together*, Caroline thought. And Matt had shared a deeply painful and personal story. Had sought her out on her birthday and taken her to dinner.

When she'd squeezed his hand to show him she was kidding about him being a criminal, she hadn't wanted to let go. Holding hands across the table with a man she'd built a long, slow relationship with this summer seemed natural—just another marker on the road she'd taken.

Except that she was digging up the surface of that road, and probably its foundation. She should be reading the report, not indulging in dinner with Matt. What if she'd finally found evidence incriminating his uncle's business? For all she knew, Matt was already aware of the contents of that report and he was entertaining her to keep her from reading it.

Looking up and meeting his green eyes, she found it hard to believe he could be hiding something treacherous. She was better at reading people than that. Wasn't she?

"Well, Nancy Drew? Are you going to tell me why it's a cop's life for you?"

"My mother wouldn't let me be a pirate. That was my first choice."

"That's everyone's first choice. What's the real reason?"

Caroline took a breath and shoved her asparagus around. It was the least tempting thing on her plate and this was her birthday. She didn't have to eat her vegetables.

But she did owe Matt a credible answer. It was only fair.

"I always want to fight for the underdog," she said. "Victims of crimes need a champion."

"Admirable."

"I hope. That's why I'm training to be a police officer."

"You could also be a lawyer. Don't they also advocate for victims?"

"They do," Caroline said. "And my mother suggested the same thing. But I feel as though lawyers are removed from the crime. They don't actually solve crimes, they just prosecute the accused." She paused and speared a piece of steak. "Someone has to do the accusing first."

"And that's where you come in," Matt said.

Caroline nodded and continued eating, hoping Matt would be satisfied with her explanation.

"I feel like there's more," he said.

So much for hoping.

"There's more to every story," Caroline said.

"And?"

She put down her fork. "When bad things happen, people deserve answers. Maybe nothing can make them feel better or replace someone they've lost, but knowing someone has been brought to justice has to help." Her words tumbled out quickly and she heard her voice rise a notch.

Why did talking to Matt unnerve her and make her want to share more than she'd shared with anyone outside her family?

Matt gave her an encouraging smile as he leaned forward and spoke quietly. "You don't have to tell me what made you feel so strongly, but I hope you'll trust me enough to give it a try."

Heat spread from her heart throughout her body. When Matt spoke to her in that low tone with thoughtfulness in every word, she considered telling him everything, even things he hadn't asked to hear.

She could at least tell him about her sister.

"When I was a baby, my older sister died in what was ruled an accident. But I've never felt it was an accident." She paused and waited for Matt to ask questions. He didn't. He reached across the table and took her hand, his eyes focused on hers, listening.

"We were staying at a hotel with my parents. Catherine was twelve, my brother, Scott, was seven, and I had just turned one.

It was a business trip for my dad, and my parents went to a company dinner with a bunch of other people who were staying in the same wing of the hotel. A fire broke out in the room next door, probably from a cigarette."

Matt's grip on her hand tightened, but he didn't say anything.

"My brother fell asleep because he was tired from playing in the hotel pool all day. Catherine took a long shower and didn't notice the smoke smell. By the time she came out of the bathroom and realized there was smoke seeping under our door, it was too late."

Matt's expression softened into concern and sympathy. Caroline took a deep breath. This was the hardest part of the story for her to tell. The part that always brought her tears to the surface. But she had to do it. Had to master her feelings if she wanted to be a police officer and help others avenge senseless deaths.

"It was too late to get out, and there were no smoke alarms or sprinklers in that hotel. No one came to our rescue, so Catherine had us all get in the bathtub with wet towels. Scott and I were on the bottom and we survived, although he has some ugly scars on his back. Catherine—" She paused and struggled to control her shaking voice. "Catherine didn't survive."

Why was it so hard for her to tell the story, especially after so many years?

"I'm so sorry," Matt said. "For you and for your family. Losing someone like that…"

"What makes me most sad is that it could have been prevented. It's why my brother became a firefighter and a fire safety inspector. It's how he copes, especially since he was old enough when it happened…he remembers."

"Was anyone ever prosecuted for failing to follow fire codes in that hotel?"

She shook her head. "It was an old building, but I don't think that's any excuse."

"Which drives you to do what you do. Make sure laws are followed."

"Yes."

"That's one of the most admirable things I've ever heard."

Just hearing Matt validate her career choice and motivation made telling the painful story worthwhile. On top of being a hard worker, loyal to his family, sweet and kind and funny, he was also a good listener. It was one of the skills she was trying to cultivate in herself.

People who lived with their ears wide-open often heard things they never expected, and sometimes didn't want to know. Did Matt know more about his family's construction business than others—even his mother and brother?

The waitress arrived, cleared their plates and asked about dessert.

"Do you have cake?" Matt asked instead of opening the dessert menu.

"Chocolate torte, white chocolate raspberry and carrot."

"Chocolate," Caroline said.

"Make that two," Matt added.

"So that wasn't the best birthday conversation," Caroline said, attempting to lighten the mood after the waitress left.

"I asked," Matt said. "And I'm glad you told me. Birthdays are a good time to look back on where you've been and think about where you're going. We broke ground on the new coaster on my birthday this past May, and it will open next year on my birthday if I don't manage to screw it up."

"You won't."

"I hope you're right."

CHAPTER FIFTEEN

AFTER DESSERT AND settling the bill—which Matt insisted on paying—Caroline and Matt walked past the boats in the marina. The sun had just set and a soft darkness enveloped them as they turned toward her dorm.

Matt reached down and took her hand as they walked. Caroline liked having her hand in his. Even though she didn't need protection, he made her feel safer than she had in a long time. Perhaps it was sharing her past. Maybe it was trusting someone enough to open her heart.

Was it so hard for her to be vulnerable? She'd spent years developing a safe wall around her emotions so they wouldn't escape and couldn't be hurt. Was there a place in that wall where a window might go?

"I had big plans for this summer," Matt said. "But I never planned on meeting someone like you."

"Someone like me?"

"I love building things. Love the sound of trucks and the feel of the dirt under my boots. I love reading blueprints and seeing walls go up, concrete being poured. That's my life. It's why I studied construction engineering. But you're the first woman I've met who makes me want to take a day off and just—"

They paused under one of the old cottonwood trees growing along the dim path that led to the employee dormitory.

"And just do this," he said. Matt ran his gentle fingers through Caroline's hair until his hand came to rest on her shoulder.

The feeling of peace and safety she'd felt strengthened. She leaned closer to him and tipped her head up, inviting him to kiss her. He lowered his head and his lips brushed hers.

It was delicious. She tasted chocolate icing on his lips, and it was the best birthday gift she'd received in a long time. She slipped her arms around his waist and returned his kiss, wishing it would go on a long time. His hands caressing a circle on her back felt almost as good as his lips.

She'd never thought she'd meet someone who would make her forget she was devoting her life to solving crimes. But here she was kissing Matt Dunbar along the waterfront and ignoring the envelope she'd waited six weeks to get.

The envelope! She'd left it on the chair next to hers in the restaurant. She pulled back from his kiss with a gasp.

"Was it that bad?" he asked.

"No," she said, laughing. "It was very good. You taste like birthday cake."

He moved his hands to her shoulders. "So you've...had enough cake for the evening?"

"I forgot something. In the restaurant. I have to run back and get it before they throw it away or it gets lost."

"Wait here, I'll run back for you."

"No," she said quickly. She didn't want him to see the return address or, worse yet, look inside. Not that she believed he would violate her privacy like that. But as the man building a roller coaster ride at an amusement park in Michigan, he would certainly recognize the name of the state agency that inspected rides. He'd probably met with them several times this summer. If he knew she had a report from them, he'd certainly put it together that her investigation into the Loose Cannon was continuing.

She wasn't sure how she felt at the moment, but she didn't want that envelope to ruin the perfect evening she'd been having. With a man who'd completely distracted her from her summer mission. Perhaps it was time to call it a night.

"Thank you for dinner," she said, slowly stepping backward, although it didn't feel right to leave the warmth of his arms.

"Thank you," Matt said. He didn't try to stop her retreat. He only kept his eyes on her. "It was the nicest evening I've had in a long time. And I hope you had a great twenty-first birthday."

"The best one I've ever had," she said.

Matt laughed.

"I should run back and get that…uh… thing I was reading."

"Do you want me to come with you? Or wait here for you?" In the dim glow from the lights in the parking area, she saw hope on his face. It was there in the way his eyebrows raised and the lines around his eyes deepened and curved.

Was this really the best night he'd had in a while? A smart, attractive man like Matt couldn't possibly have trouble finding dates, could he?

Not unless he was already married to his work.

She shook her head. "I should call it a night. Early shift tomorrow."

"I have the early shift every day. But I also have tomorrow evening free."

Was he asking her out again?

"I've been thinking about what you said the night we met," Matt said. "About how I'm building a roller coaster, but I don't usually ride them."

"I remember. I shouldn't have given you such a hard time."

"But you were right. Since we both have the early shift tomorrow, is there any chance you'll hold my hand while I try out the most thrilling coasters at Starlight Point?"

She shouldn't. But the memory of his lips on hers combined with the hopeful expression on his face made her cancel her plans—laundry—for the following night. And if she said yes quickly enough, he'd go home and let her dash back to the restaurant to reclaim the report that hadn't yielded any answers. Yet.

"If you say yes, I'll also let my crew go home an hour early. They work hard, they deserve it."

"That's very persuasive."

"I hope so. They'll be really surprised, especially since the forecast for tomorrow is perfect working weather."

Caroline hesitated. It would be fun to ride coasters with Matt. Her feelings were already going up hills and through loops.

"It's also perfect amusement park weather," Matt added.

"What time?"

"I'd like to run home to shower and change, so maybe five o'clock?"

"You didn't go home and change tonight," she said, pointing at his work clothes.

"Tonight was a special occasion. I saw someone I care about sitting alone on her birthday. It was an emergency."

Caroline laughed. "I'll meet you here tomorrow at five. Wear comfortable shoes."

Matt held out his hand, inviting her to take it. "One more kiss before I go?"

She had already taken a few backward

steps toward the restaurant, but she couldn't resist Matt. She'd been doing it all summer, and she was out of ammunition.

Caroline stepped into his arms and kissed him just long enough to be certain he'd be thinking about her until they saw each other next.

CHAPTER SIXTEEN

THE NEXT DAY at half past three, Caroline happened to look out her window and saw the construction trucks leaving the work site. She wondered if Matt had told his crew why they were starting their evening a good hour and a half before they usually did. Was he putting the job at risk by knocking off early? The thought worried her until she rationalized Matt's decision. In a year-long build, did a few hours matter?

There was no doubt building a ride was complicated. She had stayed up until nearly one in the morning trying to focus on the state report about the accident on the Loose Cannon. She was paying attention to every detail, although she had to reread a page more than once because her thoughts strayed to Matt.

And the way he kissed. And how sweet it was for him to buy her dinner and cake on

her birthday. When was the last time someone had gone out of his way to be nice to
her? Sure, the other cops were cordial and
friendly. She had friends among the seasonal
workers. The Hamilton family treated her
like a little sister.

But Matt was different. He seemed…
interested. He was five years older than she
was. Did it matter? No. Was she looking for
romance? No. But how often did someone
find what they were looking for? It was one
of the first things she'd learned about being a
detective. Sometimes unexpected clues and
good and bad surprises were right in front
of your face.

The report itself had been disappointing.
The photographs were old and their clarity
was further decimated by being photocop-
ies. The structural notes on the ride itself revealed no obvious answers, no smoking gun.
Notes indicated no mechanical problems
with the ride, no broken parts or missing
bolts. The bolts, grade eights she noticed,
were described as new. It made sense, considering the ride itself was new. Interviews
with witnesses conflicted or were dis-
counted because they were fuzzy or based

on what people had heard, not seen with their own eyes.

If the accident had happened during daylight, it might have been different. If the inspectors had arrived the night of the accident, they might have found something else. In the light of the next day, there were no obvious answers.

Could someone have altered evidence overnight? Was George Dupont there for that reason? If so, who was he protecting? Himself? Starlight Point?

Caroline had finally shoved the papers into the envelope and tried to sleep on her narrow bed in her dorm. She'd stood in the sun outside the construction zone all day, trying to stay sharp on only a few hours of sleep. She hated to admit, even to herself, how much she'd thought about Matt throughout the day.

And now she waited for him on the bench near where they had kissed the previous night. Caroline wore a butter-yellow T-shirt with a sailboat on it. It was one of her few shirts that had nothing to do with law enforcement. She wore navy blue shorts and sneakers, and had her money, employee identification and cell phone in a tiny purse she could hook to her belt loop when she went on rides.

It was almost five o'clock when she finally saw a tall blond man walking along the sidewalk on the Outer Loop road.

As she watched him approach, she noticed his blue T-shirt and khaki shorts, his broad shoulders and his confident walk. A smart, strong man, he had every reason to swing his arms and take long strides. But he'd revealed something personal last night, letting her know he wasn't acting on bravado. He, like many other people, was driven by what he wanted and what he feared he would lose. It made her like him even more than she already had.

How long had she liked him?

She had to admit it. She'd liked him since that first night when he'd offered to surrender in the beam of her flashlight.

"Don't tell me you parked in the main lot and walked all this way?" she said as he approached.

"I did. I don't have a parking permit for this lot, and I'd be lying if I said I was eating in the restaurant again. Although I enjoyed it a lot last night."

Caroline stood and hesitated. Should she give him a hug? Kiss him? Shake hands?

"And I thought it would be a lousy start to our date if you had to write me a ticket," Matt added.

He put a hand on her upper arm, touching her lightly. She moved into his embrace and loved how he smelled of shaving cream. He'd shaved for her.

"I would have let you off with a warning," she said.

"How about if I kiss you right here in the daylight where people can see? Would I get a warning for that, too?"

"You'll have to make it a quick one. If people see, I'll lose my reputation as a tough cop."

Matt kissed her, his lips soft and tender. It was quick, just as she had requested, but it left her wanting more. He took her hand and they turned toward the park. It was only a short walk across the parking lot to the entrance gate for marina guests and employees.

"Would you like to eat first or ride first?" he asked.

Caroline shot him a quizzical look. "I'm starting to think you're really serious about not riding rides."

"Why?"

"You can't eat before riding coasters. Unless you're tougher than I think you are."

"How tough do you think I am?"

"Just right," Caroline said. He could probably pick her up and carry her over his head through the marina gate. But he wasn't the kind of man who'd prove himself in that way. And that's what she liked about him.

"You should plan our itinerary," Matt said.

"Big coasters first. Then dinner. Then baby rides."

Matt laughed. "I'm following you."

Caroline dug her employee identification out of her tiny purse as they approached the gate. "Do you have a ticket or a pass?" she asked.

"Season pass. Jack gave it to me. He said his wife taught him that you have to have fun on the job sometimes and not take yourself too seriously."

"I can picture Augusta saying that. She loves her work, and so does everybody who eats her cookies and cakes. I guess it would be fun to do a job where everyone loves you."

"Everyone doesn't love police officers?" Matt asked. He handed his season pass to the girl working the turnstile.

"Depends on the situation," Caroline said. "And which side of the law they're on."

Matt put a hand on Caroline's back as they entered Starlight Point. Tall trees formed an umbrella over them, but they still heard the roller coasters overhead and the sounds of music and crowds.

"I'll make sure I stay on the right side of the law," Matt said.

"Good plan. Right now, I'm thinking of lining up for the Sea Devil. It's the largest and wildest coaster here. For now, anyway. I heard there'll be a better one next year."

"I hope."

Caroline headed straight for the entrance of the Sea Devil where a sign announced only a fifteen-minute wait. It was a weeknight, so it was a good time to ride without spending the entire night in queues. Saturdays, forget it. Caroline knew the patterns from one and a half summers of watching the crowds and lines at the Point.

"You have fifteen minutes to dread this," Caroline said.

"I have fifteen minutes to enjoy with you. Before I put my fate in a tiny steel track."

"Don't you trust these rides?"

"Tough question," he said. "Your favorite kind."

Caroline swatted him playfully on the arm. "Am I really so bad?"

"No."

As they stood in the queue winding under the structural supports of the ride, Caroline thought about the Loose Cannon. What had caused that accident? Would she ever learn the answer? She caught sight of a large electrical panel fenced and gated off from park guests. How did a man, experienced with electricity, accidentally die? And on the same night an accident claimed the life of a young girl.

There had to be more to the story. There had to be an answer. She owed it to the families of the two people who had died thirty years ago.

"You look as if you're facing down a murderer," Matt said. He leaned on the railing across from her. His large forearms rested on the metal bar and he looked relaxed.

"Are you actually afraid of riding this?" she asked. "Because you don't look it."

"I'm excellent at faking bravery. It's how I make it through every single day of doubting myself."

"You shouldn't doubt yourself."

Matt smiled and pointed above them at the complicated network of towers, track, hydraulics and wires.

"I see your point," Caroline said. "So tell me how the Sea Devil works."

"I didn't build this one, but it's much like the one I'm installing right now. Of course, we'll bring in experts when we get to the more technical issues of installing and testing track. There are companies that specialize in coasters, guys who spend their lives dreaming of tall hills, inverted loops and air time."

"But not you."

"I'm more a concrete footer and nuts and bolts guy." He pointed to a beam over them. "Mechanical and structural elements are my thing. Not the creativity part."

Caroline looked at the beam he pointed

to. Several rows of large bolts circled a joint in the beam. Most of the bolts were painted the same blue as the ride, but a few of them were shiny silver. Matt followed her glance.

"Looks like they replaced a few bolts, probably at the beginning of the season," he said.

"Why?"

"They wear. If you look closely, you'll see there are little painted marks on the bolts that line up with a painted line on the beam. That way, the maintenance guys can see if the bolts are turning with the force of the ride. If they find that, they have to address it before it causes a failure."

Caroline thought about the pictures of bolts in the file in her dorm room. They were labeled New by the state inspectors, but were there degrees of new? Were the bolts in the Loose Cannon at the time of the accident the same bolts it began the season with? If not, would there be a maintenance record documenting a change? Too bad the photographs were of such poor quality. They might have revealed something.

"Cop face again," Matt said.

Caroline laughed. "Sorry. I was thinking

about ride failure and what a nightmare that would be."

Matt's expression sobered. "It would be."

Although neither of them mentioned the Loose Cannon, Caroline would have bet her badge they were both thinking about it. It was the elephant in the room between them.

Matt's family didn't talk about it...but why not? Was it just a painful memory, something that had taken the wind out of his uncle's sails? Now that Matt's stepfather was in failing health, was it too painful to bring up?

Would opening an old wound be so shocking that it would shorten Bruce Corbin's life?

The line ahead of them moved, and Caroline and Matt walked side by side through the queues, their arms touching and hands brushing. Matt squeezed Caroline's hand and gave her a small sideways smile. His touch and his smile were much more pleasant than dredging up a dead-end case, no matter how much Caroline believed in her heart it wasn't really a dead end.

She wouldn't find the answer tonight.

They climbed the steps to the loading

platform and took their place in the holding area for the next train.

"Ladies first," Matt said when the train's lap bar released and the ride operator directed guests to enter the cars.

"You're not going to run away, are you?"

"I wouldn't think of it," he said. He plopped down in the seat next to Caroline and snugged up his seat belt. He pulled the lap bar down, but because he was so much taller, it stopped when it hit his knees. Caroline had plenty of wiggle room under the bar. "Are you sure that's safe? I could always ride with someone closer to my size."

"I was planning to hold your hand the whole time."

"Then I'm staying right where I am."

After the Sea Devil, which Matt rode without screaming once, Caroline led them toward the older wooden coaster in the Wonderful West part of the park. She and Matt had walked the Western Trail one time before, the first night they'd met.

"That's where my tent was," Matt said, pointing to a patch of grass near a saloon and gift shop.

"I was just thinking about that," Caroline said.

"Did you ever imagine you'd be having fun with a trespasser like me?"

"I have an excellent imagination. It helps me think like a criminal and will make me a better police officer."

"I don't doubt that one bit. How many more rides do I have to endure before I'm allowed to have dinner?"

"How about two?"

"I can handle two. I skipped lunch today so I could quit early, so I'm operating on the breakfast I ate at six this morning and a granola bar I found in my toolbox. I have no idea how old it was, but I'm still alive so that's a good sign."

"How about one more ride and then we'll eat amusement park food that will make that granola bar look even healthier than it probably was."

"I love you," Matt said.

Caroline drew in a quick breath and glanced up.

"Your plan," Matt said. "I love your plan."

"That's…what I thought you meant," she

såid. She laughed. "It's obviously a good one."

"I agree."

Did Matt really love her plan, or had a slice of truth slipped out in a candid moment? Caroline weighed the evidence, but she couldn't rule out the fact that there was something unexpected and wonderful happening between her and Matt.

CHAPTER SEVENTEEN

THE OLD-FASHIONED wooden coaster in the Wonderful West wasn't as thrilling as the Sea Devil, but Matt's heart was racing anyway. It had to be the company. Having Caroline next to him, her leg touching his as they were catapulted over hills and through loops, sent waves of excitement through him.

"Are you in the mood for something sweet?" Caroline asked as they exited the swinging gate at the end of the ride.

I certainly am.

"Food," she said. "Aunt Augusta's Last Chance Bakery is in the back of the park. We could get a cookie as an appetizer and then walk up front and eat on the midway."

Matt nodded. Caroline took his hand and started walking.

"I know a shortcut," she said.

"I imagine you know this park inside and out."

"Have to. Every gate, food stand, ride entrance and merchandise location. It's part of the early season training—we have to know where we're going when we get dispatched somewhere."

She led him down a deserted alley behind the Starlight Saloon. It was nearly dark and they were alone, even though there was plenty of ambient noise from the amusement park all around them. Caroline glanced up at him and the evening light cast a pink glow over her face.

Matt was thunderstruck by her beauty. He'd noticed it all summer long, but the more he knew her, the more he knew her beauty was deeper than just her exterior.

"I admire your work," he said. "Doing your best to prevent other people from making mistakes. It seems like a daunting job."

She shrugged. "No more daunting than building a multimillion-dollar roller coaster." She stopped walking and turned toward him, still holding his hand. "Thanks for having fun with me tonight. Sometimes I take myself too seriously and forget I work in the middle of what most people would consider a vacation."

"I have the same problem." *And plenty of others.*

He put his hand on her cheek and kissed her, a quick touch of lips and then a longer one. Her lips were soft and sweet, and he wondered how he was going to keep his mind on his work now that he had fallen for the police officer who stood right outside his construction fence. It could be a very long summer, especially considering how high the stakes were for him and for the future of his stepfather's company.

Matt's stomach rumbled loudly, audible even over the noise of a roller coaster in the distance.

"Cookies," Caroline said. "Right around the corner."

They crossed a wooden porch and shoved through saloon-style doors into the Last Chance Bakery.

As soon as they saw who was already there, Caroline dropped Matt's hand. Jack Hamilton and Mel Preston stood in the doorway that led to the back of the bakery, which housed the ovens and work area.

"Hey, Caroline," Jack said. And then his eyes traveled to Matt. "And Dunbar."

Matt could see Jack processing his thoughts, his expression changing from confusion to understanding.

"I'm glad to see you're out having fun," Augusta said. She wore a pink apron and two oven mitts as she appeared between her husband and brother-in-law. Augusta nudged Jack and shot him a quick glance. "We're not having so much fun in here. I have one dead oven and two men who can't seem to fix it."

"Hey," Mel said. "I just got here. Jack's the one who doesn't know what he's doing."

"Not in my job description," Jack muttered. "I just want to pick up my wife so someone will help me with bath and bedtime at home. It's easier running an amusement park than it is getting a two-year-old in bed."

"Thanks for taking a look at the oven, Mel, but I think I may need to call the manufacturer tomorrow," Augusta said. She turned to the two teenagers working the counter. "We have enough stock for the evening crowd, so I'm going home."

"We came for cookies," Caroline blurted out. She clutched her hands together in front of her body. Did she feel awkward showing up with a date and running into her brothers-in-law who were also her bosses? Or did she feel awkward because she was with him? Or both?

"Caroline decided I'd be a better roller coaster builder if I actually rode the rides that are already here," Matt said. "She made a convincing case."

"I bet she did," Mel said, grinning.

"Oven," Augusta said. "It's the new one clear in the back."

Augusta and Mel went into the back of the shop, but Jack lingered. "Anything new with the ride this week?"

Matt shook his head. He felt strangely guilty for taking off a few hours early today so he could spend time with Caroline. Jack had even more riding on this new build than Matt did because it was his park's money. What would he think about Matt being distracted by Caroline instead of working?

"On track," Matt said. "I'll give you the full update at our meeting tomorrow."

Each Friday morning, Matt visited the corporate office building tucked behind the scrambler ride and several tall old trees. The weekly report usually included good coffee, and his relationship with the Hamiltons was cordial. He'd begun to feel as if he was part of the family—which was another reason he shouldn't date someone who was, by marriage, part of the Hamilton family.

The acid in his empty stomach churned when he considered everything he was juggling. His stepfather's business, his family's future, the massive construction project and now Caroline—the best part of his complicated situation.

"Good," Jack said. He smiled. "When I was first dating Augusta three summers ago, we rode coasters together on a beautiful evening just like this. She didn't like it at first, but she took a chance on me."

Matt waited for Caroline to interject and say they weren't dating. But she didn't. He didn't, either.

Instead of answering, Matt strolled over to the glass case and evaluated his snack choices. He heard Jack say good-night to Caroline and the creak of the door to the back workroom.

"How many are you getting?" Caroline

asked, appearing next to him but not touching him.

"Half dozen maybe? That should be enough fuel to get me to wherever you're planning on having dinner in the front of the park."

Caroline pointed to the decorated sugar cookies resembling rides and iconic structures at Starlight Point. "Two carousel horses, one Sea Devil, a Lake Breeze Hotel and...what else do you like?" she asked Matt.

"Do you think they'll have a cookie shaped like the new ride next year?" he asked.

"I don't see how," she said. She squeezed his hand and relaxed her shoulders. "It'll be such a tangled mess of track, what would that look like in a cookie?"

"We just use a generic cookie cutter that looks like a hill and ice it in the signature colors of the rides," the girl behind the counter explained. "See?" She held up a Sea Devil cookie and a Silver Streak cookie. Although the Sea Devil was much newer and wilder than the venerable old Silver Streak, the cookies had the same outline and only differed in the colors of icing. "What colors will the new ride be?" she asked.

"Black and white to go with the star theme."

"Oh." The girl's expression sobered. "Black icing isn't very appetizing. Maybe we won't do a cookie for that ride."

Matt sighed. Building a new ride was definitely not all glamour.

"We'll have two of those Silver Streak cookies to finish out the half dozen," he said.

As they left the bakery and headed up the trail, Caroline held open the box for Matt to take some of the cookies. "Don't let it get to you. Just because your ride could be a potential failure as a sugar cookie does not mean you should stay awake worrying about it."

"Who says I was going to do that?" he asked, smiling and then biting off a wing of the Lake Breeze Hotel.

"I think I have you figured out by now."

"I'd be worried if I didn't know you have hound-dog-detective blood in your veins."

Instead of walking up the Western Trail on their way to the front midway, Caroline chose a louder and more crowded route that wound past several midsize roller coasters and family fun rides. The cookies were gone before they crossed the railroad tracks for the authentic steam train that circled the Point dozens of times every day.

It was too noisy for conversation, and Matt was happy to stroll along in the evening air with Caroline by his side. They held hands most of the way, only separating to make room for a large family group including a wheelchair and three strollers.

When they reached the midway, Matt smelled fried food. He glanced over at Caroline.

"I know what you're thinking. Again," she said.

"Despite your talent in that department, it can't be too hard to figure out. Do you smell those fries?"

She nodded and laughed. "Burgers and fries right this way."

They lined up, ordered food and carried their plastic trays to a picnic table outside near the midway carousel. The painted horses circled in front of them, cable cars slid past over their heads and music poured from the loudspeakers. Guests of all ages streamed past on their way to fun.

Matt remembered coming here with his family when he was about seven. His brother was in a stroller and his parents took turns pushing it. It was from a time in his life before he and everyone else found out his father was a criminal.

"We came here when I was a kid," he said. "Bought two-day tickets, stayed overnight and made a vacation out of it. I thought it was the best thing ever."

"Me, too," Caroline said. "We came once a summer. We only lived an hour away so we didn't stay over. I used to love the cars and motorcycles in Kiddie Land until I realized they were on a track and I wasn't actually driving. It was a huge disappointment."

"I liked the fountain," Matt said. He pointed down the midway to a large water feature with a big rubber splash pad. On the warm summer evening, children ran through it while their parents held their shoes and watched. "That's one of the things I remember from that trip. It was really hot, and my mom let me take off my shoes and run through the water. My clothes got soaked, but it felt so good."

"Did you just come once?"

"At that time, yes, but when my mom remarried and we moved to Bayside, I came over fairly often just like most of the local kids. My senior prom was in the ballroom and afterward we got to change clothes and ride the coasters in the dark."

"Did you actually ride them?"

He shook his head. "My date left early with her friends and most of the guys took coolers of beer to the beach."

Caroline raised both eyebrows at him.

"I went for a while, but I had to work the next day. Construction happens on Sundays, too, when the weather is good. We were putting up roof beams and I remember how hot it was and how glad I was not to be hungover."

"Did your stepdad set that up on purpose?"

"Maybe. He's got a strong work ethic and he expects it of everyone else, too. That's how he took a business that was nearly defunct and turned it into what it is now. And it's also why he wants to make a careful choice about its future."

"Why was the business failing?" Caroline asked.

Maybe he shouldn't have brought it up. Matt shrugged. "My uncle was a good builder, but after the failure of the Loose Cannon, he seemed to lose his enthusiasm for the business. He took on some jobs he didn't finish, started to get a bad reputation. Reputation matters in construction. If someone hears anything bad about your company, no way are you getting future contracts."

"So Bruce Corbin bailed his brother out by buying it?"

"I guess you could say that. He bought the building and equipment, changed the name and has spent the last almost thirty years building it up."

Matt wondered if Caroline would let his explanation go at that. In truth, he didn't know that his uncle's business was technically failing. He'd always assumed that from the broken pieces of dialogue he'd heard. And it was a logical explanation. Could there be another one?

Caroline ate her burger and fries instead of pressing him, and the warm summer evening in the shadow of the cable cars and carousel seemed almost too good to be true. Especially because his heart felt lighter than it had in a long time.

"DESSERT?" CAROLINE ASKED.

Matt laughed. "We had cookies before we ate dinner, so I think we're covered. Unless you talk me into ice cream later."

"I'll try."

They disposed of their food trays and gave up their table to a group of teenagers carrying cotton candy, ice cream cones and sodas.

"Where to next?" Matt asked.

"Anywhere. We hit the best coasters and ate junk food, so anything else we do tonight is bonus."

"Carousel? We're right here."

"We could be more adventurous and ride the cable cars," Caroline suggested. "It's one notch up on the thrill rating and it'll be fun to have an aerial view of the Point as all the lights are coming on."

They climbed the steps to the cable car loading platform. Caroline was thinking about whether she'd sit across from Matt in the car or next to him. Would he put his arm around her?

So far, the evening had been sweet and fun. Much better than any other one she'd had at Starlight Point. Would it end in another kiss? She had to admit it, she was falling for Matt Dunbar. And she didn't need to be a detective to know he felt the same way.

Two maintenance men were on the platform of the cable car loading area as Matt and Caroline approached, but they appeared to be finished with whatever brought them there. Tool bags over their shoulders, they were sidestepping the people coming up the staircase.

"Hey, Caroline," one of them said.

She nodded and smiled at Noah, one of the year-round maintenance men just a few years older than she was. She lowered her voice and leaned close. "Is it a bad sign that you're here? Would you advise us to come back later? Or bring a parachute?"

"No," he said. "Everything's fine or they wouldn't run the ride. We were replacing one of the shields over the cables. Not so much a safety concern. It's mostly just for looks."

As he spoke, his partner knelt, picked up a broken bolt and tucked it in his pocket. Caroline stared at the man and a chill washed over her. The maintenance man who had died under the Loose Cannon the night of the accident had a broken bolt in his pocket.

She realized she was staring when Noah interrupted her thoughts. "He's not stealing anything, officer. It was just a broken bolt. We twisted it off when we were replacing the shield, but you don't want to leave things lying around. People get nervous if they see stuff like that. They might think it's not safe."

Caroline wanted to smile. Wanted to laugh or shrug or indicate in some way that it was no big deal, but thoughts were racing through her brain and she felt a strange combination of exhilaration and ice-cold foreboding.

Did the broken bolt in George Dupont's pocket mean nothing at all? If so, her investigation was back to square one.

But what if the broken bolt was the key to the whole mystery...what if it were something worth killing for?

"OUR TURN TO get on," Matt said, interrupting Caroline's thoughts as the maintenance men descended the stairs and disappeared. "What's the matter? Don't you want to ride?"

Caroline managed to nod and followed

Matt into one of the cable cars, the door of which was being held open by a ride operator in a red-and-blue uniform. She sat next to Matt. Only a few moments ago, she'd looked forward to Matt putting his arm around her. But now she sat beside him so he couldn't see her face when she turned away.

The car descended the short hill out of the station and swung free, suspended only by the cable overhead, as it made its way down the midway. Matt did put his arm around her shoulders, but Caroline couldn't think about it. Couldn't think about the warmth of his touch and how much she had thought she wanted it.

She was thinking about that broken bolt, and a hypothesis presented itself as if it were written in neon lights on the midway below. Someone—she didn't yet know who—had been there the night of the accident. Had replaced something broken on the Loose Cannon. And had left behind a piece of evidence. A broken number five bolt.

And there was only one explanation. She'd previously thought Starlight Point might be covering its tracks, but now it became clear. The construction company was the one with something to hide. If they had used grade five bolts to save money, and if those bolts sheered off…a fatal accident could occur. If they slipped in under cover of darkness before the state agency arrived the next day, they could replace the grade five bolts with stronger ones—grade eights like Mel was using that day on the Scrambler—and no one would be the wiser.

Unless someone caught them. And picked up a piece of evidence. And then died with that evidence in his pocket.

"You're awfully quiet," Matt said.

"Just thinking."

"Ride's almost over." Matt pointed to the end of the cable car line, which they were rapidly approaching.

Caroline desperately wanted off the ride so she could continue developing her theory. If she was right, the maintenance man's death was no accident. Whoever didn't want him to talk would have had every reason to kill, especially with thousands of dollars, a company reputation and an accidental death on their hands.

Did John Corbin's company get caught

in a cover-up and kill to keep it quiet? Did Matt know?

Caroline followed Matt out of the cabin as if she were a zombie. He took her hand as they descended the stairs onto the midway.

It was completely dark now and the lights were on all over Starlight Point. The roller coaster hills were illuminated, and marquee lights on the restaurants flashed. It was pretty and familiar, but Caroline was glad for the darkness. She didn't think she could conceal the grim expression on her face as she thought about the decades-old crime.

"My brother's stand is still open," he said. "And he doesn't have a line. We could stop and say hello."

"Sure," Caroline said. If Matt wanted to chat with his brother, maybe she could keep her thoughts to herself. Why hadn't the state agency noticed some of the bolts were newer than others? Didn't they suspect the construction company or Starlight Point might want to cover their tracks, especially when they were dealing with a fatality?

She had to get home and examine those photographs again. Would any difference in the bolts be visible in old photocopied pictures?

"Hey, Caroline," Agnes said as soon as Caroline and Matt entered the circle of light cast by the caricature booth. "You're not wearing your uniform, so do I finally get the chance to draw you wearing an evening gown? It's a slow night here. Everyone wants cotton candy instead of caricatures." She pointed to the long line at a nearby food stand.

"You could draw my brother," Lucas said. "I already took a shot at it, and I've had to look at him my whole life."

"Why not draw us together?" Matt asked. He pointed to the sample drawings, many of which contained couples or siblings.

Caroline considered objecting, but it would be a good opportunity for her to think without making conversation. She thought she could manage to fake a smile despite the turmoil in her mind.

"Okay," she said.

A mom with two little girls entered the booth. "I'll do those three," Agnes said. "But, Lucas, you better not make Caroline a cop in your drawing."

Caroline and Matt sat next to each other in front of Lucas's easel. "You don't have to smile, but it sure makes for a better picture," Lucas said.

Matt smiled broadly and put his hand on Caroline's knee. She tried to return his smile, tried to bring back the feelings she'd had earlier in the evening as they'd enjoyed the rides, the food and each other's company. It wasn't fair to Matt that her thoughts were occupied by the Loose Cannon.

Or was it? Did he know his uncle's company could be involved in a cover-up?

If he knew and was concealing it, he was an expert in deception. And she found that hard to believe based on what she knew of him so far. She should try to enjoy the rest of the evening, if only to avoid revealing her suspicions before she was ready. In her heart, though, she knew that even if Matt had no knowledge of the accident and murder, she would hurt him if she continued her investigation.

She would have to throw away the feelings she'd been developing for him all summer. The way she loved it when he smiled and the way his hard hat left an indentation around his head. The way he treated others and cared about them…especially her. She glanced sideways at Matt.

"That's better," Lucas said when Caroline returned Matt's smile. "I already know all about my brother, but you should give me some ideas—things you like that I could include in your caricature."

"And you can't say police work," Matt said.

"Why not? Your brother already drew you doing your construction job."

"Yes, and that's why he's going to do something different tonight."

"Never mind," Lucas said, grinning. "I'll use my imagination."

Caroline sat very still, trying to maintain a smile and trying hard not to think about Matt's warm hand on her knee. It felt so right, and she had enjoyed being with him so much. But she owed it to the murdered maintenance man—she was almost sure it was murder now—and the elderly parents of the young girl who was killed. She had to question Bruce Corbin, no matter how painful it would be for him. And for Matt.

The truth was more important than her

summer romance, even though it had remained buried for thirty years. Wasn't it?

Agnes walked behind Lucas's easel, glanced at the drawing and laughed.

"I'm almost afraid to see this," Matt commented.

"Just a few more minutes," Lucas said. He continued selecting pastels from his tray and shading in colors. "You can stop smiling now," he added.

"Not sure I can," Matt said. He leaned a little closer to Caroline and their shoulders brushed. She smiled despite herself, despite her thoughts.

"Ready?" Lucas asked. He took the paper off his easel and held it up for them.

The drawing showed Caroline pinning Matt to the ground with one hand while his arms and legs flailed. She was dressed as a queen, in a huge purple gown with a gold crown. Matt, however, was dressed as a clown with a silly hat, multicolored costume and giant shoes.

"It's drawn from a real-life experience," Lucas explained. "The self-defense class you had to crawl home from."

Matt glanced at Caroline and she knew

he was remembering the same thing she was. He hadn't crawled home after that class. They'd gone on their first date and he'd opened his heart about his father. Just like she'd opened her heart at her birthday dinner. Now she wondered if it had been a good idea at all, considering the way she was planning to betray their relationship.

"That's not exactly how I remember it," Matt said.

"I think it's an accurate portrayal of the STRIPE class," Caroline protested. "Except for the clown costume."

"He's supposed to be a court jester," Lucas said. "Not the same as a clown. The court jester serves at the pleasure of the queen and amuses her no matter how serious she looks."

"At least she doesn't look like a cop," Agnes commented from behind her easel. "So why is your brother a court jester?"

"Because he's really quite serious, but he tries to use humor to cover it up."

"Am I that transparent?" Matt asked.

Caroline wondered if Matt was completely transparent. Had he shared everything he knew about the Loose Cannon?

Was his reason for avoiding the topic really his stepfather's health?

Either way, she needed to find a way to end this date because she was facing a horrible choice. She could betray Matt by going behind his back to investigate JC Construction, or she could betray her beliefs by letting the case go.

Both of those options would break her heart.

CHAPTER EIGHTEEN

"DID I SCREW UP?" Matt asked. He walked next to Caroline on the way back to the employee dormitory. Their evening had been going so well, he'd wished he could freeze his summer in time. Until something between them seemed to shift and break the spell. "You've been pretty quiet since the cable cars."

"And that worries you?"

"It makes me wonder what you're thinking. Am I the worst date you've had in your life?"

"No," she said. "Definitely not."

"That's a relief."

They passed through the turnstiles and waited for cars on the Outer Loop to pass by. It was closing time, and traffic snaked in a long line past the marina and out through the parking lot.

"You'll be stuck in traffic," Caroline said.

"And you're probably getting up early to-morrow."

It was nice of her to think of him, but he'd gladly sit in horn-honking traffic all night just for a few more magical hours with her. He shrugged one shoulder in response. "I don't mind. Even if I got home in the next five minutes, I wouldn't be able to go to sleep for hours anyway."

"Worried about your work?"

"Not tonight. My mind is on something else." Did he dare tell her how he felt?

When a break in the line of cars allowed them to cross the road, Matt put an arm around Caroline and pulled her close as they covered the last few steps toward her dorm. He loved having her by his side. It made him feel as if anything were possible. Building a complicated ride, securing his family's future, overcoming the past…and even falling in love.

"I had fun tonight. You make me feel as if the weight of the world isn't hanging over me. Despite your tough outside, you're fun. And sweet. And I love being with you."

That confession had taken all the bravery Matt had built up from running construction equipment, climbing to the top of tall buildings and taking the chances necessary to run a business. He held his breath. Did she feel the same way?

She stopped walking and turned toward him. He could barely see her face because tall trees outside her dorm's entrance spread their leaves over the lights. Her eyebrows were drawn tight together and she put her hands in the pockets of her shorts, even though she didn't shrug off his arm that was still around her.

"I love being with you, too," she said. "But I'm not sure where we're going."

"Who says we have to go anywhere?" Matt asked. "We can keep enjoying the summer, just like this."

He wanted to kiss her. Wanted to feel her arms around him. He wanted to pull her closer, but he was afraid he'd drive her away right now if he tried.

"When the summer ends," she said, "I'll join the police academy. You'll be busy all winter building the Shooting Star. Things will be different."

"They don't have to be. We'll both be in Bayside. And even if you don't want to go out with me anymore, I'll still look for you around every corner. I'll still wish I could tell you about my day at the end of every day. I've never felt this way about someone before, and I'll admit it scares me," Matt said.

"It scares me, too," Caroline whispered.

Matt knew how much it cost Caroline to admit she was afraid of something, anything. Even if she didn't say anything more tonight, those words were enough for him to know he'd claimed at least a piece of her heart.

"Good-night kiss?" he asked.

The line between her brows faded and she smiled. When their lips touched, Matt knew he wouldn't be able to let her go, even when snow blanketed Bayside. Even if they both worked twenty-three hours a day. There was something between them that couldn't be defined or defeated.

"Are you busy tomorrow night?" he asked.

"My parents are coming for birthday dinner."

"Then I'll have to survive on one more kiss until I see you again," he said.

They kissed, said good-night, and Matt

walked the long way to the back of the parking lot where his truck waited. He was halfway there when he remembered he was still carrying the plastic bag that contained their caricature.

He considered running it back to Caroline, but he didn't know where her room was. And he hoped to see her soon. He would give it to her then.

"It's YOUR DAY OFF," the police chief commented. "I didn't expect to see you scanning those ancient files."

Caroline shrugged. "I don't have plans until later. My parents are coming to take me out for a birthday dinner."

"It's your birthday?"

"It was. A few days ago. I'm twenty-one now, an age I've been waiting for."

"So you can buy your boss a drink?"

She laughed. "No, so I can tell my boss I'm officially eligible for the police academy he's in charge of."

Chief Walker swiveled in his office chair, making a slow circuit. His white shirt pulled tight across his belly and deep lines funneled down his cheeks. Caroline wondered how much longer he'd want to be chief of the Starlight Point Police Department. He'd already put in thirty years, but then again it was a pretty tame and stress-free police department to run. Generally. Only once or twice a season was there much drama— as she was discovering by wading through years of records and scanning the reports.

"You know you've had my recommendation since last year. You're a great non-bonded officer, but you'll be even better when you finish the academy and qualify for a city department."

He made another slow circle in his chair, a habit whenever something troubled or perplexed him.

"Have you continued digging around the Loose Cannon incident—the one from long before you were born?" he asked.

She wondered if he emphasized the *long before you were born* part to imply that it was so long ago it wasn't worth worrying about.

How much should she reveal? She'd stayed up late analyzing the pictures in the state report. Again. Did the bolts in one picture look any newer than another? It was hard to tell with the quality of the photographs, but way past midnight, using the magnifying app on her smart phone, she'd found something interesting in one of the pictures. A close-up of the support beam in the area of the accident showed chipped paint around a set of bolts.

Could the paint have chipped off because the bolts were changed? There were shiny new bolts on the beam, but was it possible they'd been put there the night before?

"I have," she admitted. Might as well rip off the Band-Aid. "I sent a records request to the state department of commerce for their official reports on the accident. And I've talked to key people who may know something."

"Anything else you've done to investigate?"

Her pulse hammered in her throat. She didn't want to incriminate herself by talking about her trip to personnel unless she had to. "The records here are missing."

"I know."

"Do you know where they are?"

The chief did a slow circle before coming to rest facing her. "They were officially loaned out over the winter."

Caroline wanted to ask, but she was afraid she wasn't going to like the answer. She swallowed, waiting for the chief to explain.

"Bruce Corbin said his records of the old ride were incomplete and he needed information in that file to help him write up the bid for the new one."

The floor beneath her feet dropped several inches. Bruce Corbin took that file. Why? She couldn't think of a single innocent reason. And she didn't believe that nonsense about needing information for the new bid.

"I noticed you've developed a...uh... working relationship with Matt Dunbar. And I assume you've figured out by now that he's related to the builders of the Loose Cannon."

Caroline nodded and tried to sound businesslike and knowledgeable. "His stepfather's brother, John Corbin, owned JC Construction. But he sold it after the accident. Sold it to his brother, Bruce, who renamed the company."

"And has Matt told you anything else?"

The way he asked the question made Caroline wonder if the chief really did know more about the accident. But if he did, why had he remained silent?

"He told me they don't talk about it in their family."

"Why not?"

"Because it's a sore subject. John Corbin was apparently devastated by the failure of the ride and the job of dismantling it. That's why he moved away and ran a much smaller business somewhere else until he died last winter. Matt's stepfather, Bruce, is also in bad health...so Matt doesn't want to open an old wound."

Chief Walker hoisted himself from his chair and leaned on the filing cabinet Caroline was sorting through. He lowered his voice. "I don't think you believe that whole story."

Caroline swallowed and slid the drawer closed. She looked her chief in the eye. "I don't," she said.

"And what have you found out about the death of George Dupont? I doubt that was in the ride investigation from the state."

"It wasn't."

Caroline knew she had to tell the truth no

matter how quickly it could destroy her career and all her hopes.

"So I looked in his personnel file. I accessed the information without permission."

The chief shifted his gaze to the worn surface of his desk for a moment before he closed his office door.

Caroline braced herself for the worst.

"I'm not ordering you to tell me what you've figured out, but I'm free for the next half hour if you'd like to try out a hypothesis on me. Consider it an interview for the police academy."

It was the last thing she expected him to say. All summer long, she'd had the impression that the chief wanted to let sleeping dogs lie. He hadn't encouraged her sleuthing, but he'd also done nothing to stand in her way—aside from an early warning to be careful.

Caroline walked over to her messenger bag and pulled out the state report.

The chief sat in his chair and rolled up to his desk. Caroline took the chair across from him and spread out the report. Over the next twenty minutes, she methodically presented her story of what she thought had happened that night.

The chief listened intently, only asking a few questions for clarification. Finally, he pushed back in his chair. "It's quite a story," he said. "And it holds water in theory. But where's your proof?"

The million-dollar question. She had no more proof than the investigation had found three decades ago.

"No proof," she admitted. "But I do know of one more potential witness to interview."

The chief rubbed his eyes with his thumb and forefinger. "Bruce Corbin," he said quietly. "You think he knows something and kept it to himself all these years?"

"Maybe. Maybe it's even worse than that."

"You think he might've been there the night of the alleged cover-up."

Caroline's heart was in her throat. She hated to even say it out loud. "It's possible." She took a deep breath for bravery. "It's even possible he's the murderer. If you look only at the evidence, it's clear that he's the one who benefited most in the long run by buying his brother's company at a bargain price, renaming it and building it into his own successful company with his brother out of the way."

"Hell of an accusation," the chief commented.

"It is," Caroline said. "And for once in my life, I hope I'm wrong."

"The important question is…what will you do if you're right?"

Caroline leaned back in her chair and stared at her feet. What if she was right? What if Bruce Corbin's company truly was built on a crime, on a lie? What if the company Matt dreamed of inheriting had a dark history?

Did she want to bring everything to light and risk destroying Matt's family and his future? It would kill him. Having a father in prison had devastated him and his brother. It was clear that Matt had been trying to rise above his father's actions. What would he and Lucas do if the stepfather they loved and believed in turned out to be no better than their real father? *What if his crime was far worse?*

By the time Caroline's brother picked her up to drive into Bayside for dinner with their parents, Caroline had spent hours considering the pros and cons of furthering an investigation with the power to answer old questions...and destroy futures.

"Why are you wearing your grouchy cop face?" Scott asked as he leaned across the seat and shoved open the passenger door of his pickup truck. "It's supposed to be a party."

Caroline got in the truck and clicked on her seat belt. "Maybe I don't want to be a cop."

Scott had started to back out of the parking space in front of her dorm, but he pulled back in and shut off the engine. "Start talking."

"I always wanted to solve crimes. Bring people to justice."

"And now?"

"Now I wonder if it's more complicated than I thought."

"Everything is more complicated than you think it is when you're a kid," Scott said. "Should I start handing out big brother career advice? I think water-skiing instructor is still a viable option."

Caroline sighed and cracked her knuckles until Scott reached over and squeezed both her hands in one of his. "You're really serious," he said. "What happened?"

"Remember that case I was planning to investigate involving the Loose Cannon?"

He nodded. "Did you hit a dead end?"

"Worse. I think I know what actually happened."

"You should be celebrating then."

She shook her head.

"Unless you don't like what you found out," he added.

"I don't like what I found out. At least, what I think I found out."

"Does this have anything to do with Matt Dunbar?"

"Yes," she said quietly. Caroline nearly let tears loose. She could be tough with everyone except her brother. No one understood her or cared for her more.

"He likes you a lot."

Caroline glanced over at her brother. "What makes you say that?"

"He told me so. I met with him today to go over some of the fire code issues we have to address."

"What exactly did he say?"

"We talked about the fire lane around the structure and the placement of hydrants."

Caroline jabbed her brother in the ribs. "About me," she said. "What did he say about me?"

"Oh, that. He said he liked you more than any girl he'd ever met and asked me if I minded if he dated my little sister."

"Are you kidding me?"

"No."

"Well, I wish you were. Because it's from medieval times, asking a man's permission to date someone. It's ridiculous. I can make my own decisions."

"So you like him?"

Caroline let out a long breath. "We're going to be late to dinner."

"They'll get wine while they wait for us. You have to tell me what your big dilemma is so I don't accidentally say something stupid in front of Mom and Dad which will force you to kill me later. I have a lot to live for these days."

Caroline turned to face her brother and rubbed her hands together.

"You know I've suspected all along that the accident had an actual cause, even though it was officially labeled undetermined. Nothing is undetermined. Someone had to know something."

"And that someone is…"

"The construction company that built it."

"So how did the construction company cause the accident?" he asked.

"Faulty bolts. I think they used grade five bolts to cut corners. It caused part of the structure to shift. And they came in late that night and changed the bolts in that part of the ride to grade eights."

"Do you have any evidence?"

"Not exactly. The pictures from the state ride inspection agency show new grade eight bolts, but they didn't note anything odd about it because the whole ride was only two months old. The bolts may have all looked new."

"So what led you to this conclusion?"

"The maintenance man who died of a supposed electrocution had a broken grade five bolt in his pocket."

Scott leaned back into his seat and let out a low whistle.

Caroline rested her elbow on the doorframe and looked out the window. "I keep thinking about the Knights down the street from Mom and Dad's house."

"And you feel that you owe them an explanation. Some closure."

Caroline nodded. "Yes."

"And you think that will help them cope with their daughter's death?"

"Obviously. Everyone needs closure. Everyone wants justice."

Scott reached over and touched Caroline's shoulder. "I'm not so sure about that. It was a long time ago. Don't you think they've found a way to deal with it by now? Even if they never know exactly why the ride failed… isn't the result the same?"

"I thought about that," Caroline admitted. "I even considered dropping the whole thing. John Corbin is dead. Bruce Corbin has serious health problems. The sins of that generation, maybe they should just be buried, too."

"Is that your reason for wanting to drop it?"

Caroline sighed. "Did you know Matt's real dad is serving prison time for embezzlement? And Matt hopes to inherit Bayside

Construction from the man he thinks of as his father, his role model."

"So it would kill him to find out Bruce Corbin's role in the cover-up. Assuming there was a role."

"Either way, it's damaging to the company," she said, "especially since they're building the new ride. Imagine what that would look like in the newspaper."

"So what are you going to do?"

"I wish I knew."

"Earlier this summer," Scott said slowly, "when we talked about this, I tried to make you see that finding justice for someone else is admirable, but it won't heal old wounds. At least not always. Our sister, Catherine…"

"I know," Caroline said. She swiped at a tear. "Do you think I'm taking this too far?"

"I can't tell you what to do, Caroline, although I wish I knew. We should get going or our parents will wonder where we are. And we have a twenty-first birthday to celebrate."

Caroline put her seat belt back on and watched the scenery pass on their way downtown. She tried to lighten her mood, but all she could think about was the fact that the sweet older couple down the street had never gotten to see their daughter turn twenty-one.

CHAPTER NINETEEN

CAROLINE HAD PREPARED her lines. She'd rehearsed what to say to Bruce Corbin all the way to the Bayside Construction office. Her palms were sweaty on the steering wheel when she parked in the side lot at the downtown construction office. Her steps were heavy.

Was she doing the right thing? Betraying Matt by going behind his back to question his ailing stepfather about a decades-old accident and a very recent hypothesis... It was nuclear. And it would mean the end of her relationship with Matt.

Was she willing to sacrifice that? She hesitated before she walked into the building. She didn't have to go in there. Didn't have to go through with it. The only person forcing her to go on was herself. Her belief that people deserved answers. George Dupont had no family, none that were still living.

But even in the grave, didn't he deserve the truth to be known? And Jenny…she did have family.

Caroline knew firsthand how important it was to put a family tragedy to rest. Was this what her investigation was about? Facing her own family demons? Maybe her brother was right.

She almost got back in her car and put the whole thing on ice. But a car pulled in next to hers and Bruce Corbin got out.

"Good morning," he said congenially. Despite his gray features and stooped shoulders, Caroline could see that he was once a strong and robust man. Strong enough to kill someone? It was hard to keep that thought in her head when he was smiling at her and squinting against the bright morning sunshine.

"I believe I know you," he said. "My son pointed you out on the day of the media cruise about the new ride. And, maybe I'm not supposed to say this, but he's mentioned you more than once since then. Got a picture of you on his desk inside."

Great.

"I'm Caroline Bennett," she said, holding out her hand. "I'm on the police department at Starlight Point, and that's where I met Matt." She didn't know if she should use the expression *your son* even though Bruce had called him that.

The questions she had prepared in her mind now seemed cruel in the face of Bruce's kindness. But maybe he was intentionally deflecting, trying to throw her off.

"I wonder if you might have a moment to talk," Caroline said. "I'm doing a research project about a former ride at Starlight Point, and I think you may have some insight about it."

Bruce's color paled even more and Caroline knew she'd hit a nerve. She should feel triumphant, but that wasn't the emotion rattling her nerves.

"You can come inside," he said. He walked over and held the office door for her.

Even if I left now, the damage is done. Matt would know I stopped by, and he'd know why. I might as well get the information I came for since I risked it all already.

"Thank you," Caroline said. She followed him into the air-conditioned office.

Waited while he greeted a woman at the front desk, and followed him down a short hall. They passed an open office. Matt's office, perhaps? She knew what picture he had to have on his desk. It must be the caricature from their date in the park. She was tempted to peek into his office, just out of curiosity, but Bruce was holding open a brown-paneled door.

He shut the door behind her and motioned to a chair across from his desk.

"You want to ask me about the Loose Cannon," he said. He folded his hands over his belly and kept a neutral expression on his face. "Go ahead."

"Your brother's company built it. JC Construction."

"Correct."

"And there was an accident its first season in 1985."

"Very unfortunate one. A young girl was killed," Bruce affirmed.

"Do you know what caused the accident?"

His calm expression fluttered a little and he took a deep, rattling breath before he answered. "If you're investigating it, I assume you've read the reports."

"I have."

"And the reports and investigation at the time did not determine a cause," Bruce said.

Caroline was about to ask if Bruce's brother had shared anything with him, but she heard a familiar voice in the hallway greeting the secretary and footsteps stopping right outside the door of Bruce Corbin's office.

MATT HATED LEAVING the construction site in the middle of the morning, but he needed blueprints from his office. As he drove his truck into the parking lot at Bayside Construction, there was an unexpected vehicle in the lot. A retired police car. *Caroline's car*. His first thought was that she'd come to see him at work and warmth started to spread through his chest.

For a moment. And then cold reality settled in his stomach. Caroline had to know he wouldn't be at his office. He was at the construction site every single morning.

She wasn't here to see him.

Matt slammed the door of his truck, dreading what he'd find inside. Bruce's car was also in the lot. What if he'd called and asked his stepfather to bring those documents over? It would have prevented Caroline from questioning him today, but it wouldn't stop her tomorrow. Or the next day.

He felt betrayal like a lump blocking his throat. He had specifically asked Caroline not to bother Bruce with her investigation. When he swung through the front door and said hello to his secretary, he almost expected to hear raised voices. The door to Bruce's office was closed. Matt hesitated a moment, and then he squared his shoulders and knocked.

His stepfather called to him to come in and Matt turned the doorknob, knowing what he'd find but still hoping he might be wrong.

He wasn't.

Caroline sat across from Bruce. The older man looked ashen and flustered. Caroline's lips were parted and her cheeks pink.

"Caroline," Matt said. He tried to keep his voice level. Perhaps there was some explanation other than the obvious. "What brings you here?"

She opened her mouth to speak, but no words came out.

"She came to see me," Bruce said, his voice shakier than usual. Matt gave him an assessing glance. Should he call the doctor? "Had some questions about a project my brother's company built years ago. The Loose Cannon," he added, even though there was no doubt in Matt's mind.

"Is that right?" Matt said, replying to his stepfather but looking straight at Caroline.

"I was just about to tell her I don't know anything about it, except for what's in the official reports. Which she's already read."

Matt stood just inside the door. Had it been another time and place, he might have approached Caroline. Kissed her, even. But she was doing the unforgivable. Questioning a man he'd told her was ill. Doing it behind his back. Possibly even using information he'd shared with her.

Why had he shared so much? Had she only used their relationship to get information?

The thought left a trail of ice throughout Matt's chest, pain mixing with betrayal.

"Then I guess she should go," Matt said. "We have work to do."

Caroline stood. "Matt, I—"

"Goodbye," he said.

"Why don't you walk our visitor to her car?" Bruce suggested. "And then we'll get back to work."

If Matt hadn't respected his stepfather so much, he would have refused. Instead, he held the office door for Caroline. On the way past his office, he ducked in and grabbed the caricature from his desk. "You can take this," he said, handing it to Caroline. "I had no idea how true it was until now."

He hated to admit that Caroline had him by the throat. How she seemed to hold all the power. The secretary raised both eyebrows at Matt's caustic tone. Matt knew he'd have to explain later, but he needed to pull himself together first.

When they were in the parking lot, the bright sun reflecting off the concrete and blinding them, Matt followed Caroline to her car. He had no idea what to say.

Caroline leaned on her car door and crossed her arms over her chest. She still held the caricature in one hand.

"I'm sorry," she said.

Matt laughed. "Sorry? I don't even know what you're apologizing for. Maybe for letting me make a fool of myself?"

"No." She drew her eyebrows together and her lips quivered. "You didn't make a fool of yourself."

"Right now it sure seems like I did. Like you were using me for information."

His voice shook with emotion and he knew he was in danger of saying things out of anger. But when his family was threatened, there was nothing he wouldn't do to protect them.

"I was never using you," she said. "Everything I said to you was real."

"And now you've got what you want and your little summer project will be a success."

"How dare you belittle my investigation?" she said. "People died because of that accident. They deserve justice. I told you all along that was my goal."

"Did you think I was hiding evidence? Did you think so little of me—of us—that you chose to go behind my back and confront a dying man?"

Caroline's lips parted and her eyes glistened with tears. Instead of answering him, she opened her car door and tossed the caricature onto the passenger seat.

"You know that girl who died on the ride your uncle built?" she asked. Hands on hips, she didn't even swipe away the tear that rolled down her cheek. "She was the daughter of my neighbors. A sweet older couple I grew up knowing. But they never got to see their daughter grow up."

Matt stepped back and his face felt numb. He and Caroline had never talked about the girl who died, at least not directly. His family seldom spoke of it, either. It was a sad footnote to the topic whenever it came up and was quickly squelched.

"Her name was Jenny," Caroline said. "She was only twelve. She would have been in the seventh grade when that summer ended."

Matt drew a deep breath.

"Only twelve," Caroline repeated. "The same age my sister was when she died."

"I'm sorry," Matt said. His shoulders sank. What could he say? "It was a horrible accident. The fire that took Catherine's life."

Caroline glanced up sharply when he used

her sister's name. Maybe she was surprised he remembered it, but he remembered everything about the time he'd spent with Caroline that summer.

"And the accident that killed Jenny," he continued, careful to use her name and personalize his words. "I'm sorry about them both."

Caroline stared at the ground for a moment and then up at the sky. Matt was afraid to ask what she was thinking. Her face was hard, the soft lines and tears gone and replaced by fury and resignation.

"Ask yourself how sorry you really are," she said. "Because if you are, you should go in there and ask your stepfather what he knows about that accident. Ask him about the broken number five bolt in the pocket of the maintenance man who was murdered that night."

She fished car keys from her pocket, opened her car door and got in. She rolled down her window. "Go inside and ask him," she said. "Maybe you'd rather hear it from him than from me."

"Caroline," Matt said. He laid a hand on the frame of her open window. He didn't want to let her go. Not only because she clearly knew something devastating—or at least suspected it strongly enough to betray him—but also because he desperately wanted to go back to the way things were just a few nights ago. Their date had ended with a kiss and a promise of many more summer nights under the stars.

Or so he had thought. He remembered her silence at the end of their date, her reluctance to commit to dating him. Had something changed that night or had she been reluctant all along? If he was a fool, it was his own doing, not hers. But the result was the same.

He couldn't find any words, even though Caroline waited for a long moment before starting her car.

"Go ask him," she said. "You know where to find me if you want to talk about this."

Matt watched her drive away, feeling as if someone had taken the hammer out of his toolbox and used it to smash his heart.

When he turned toward the doorway of the construction office, he saw Bruce holding the door open. The old man had tears in his eyes, and Matt knew he was about to hear something that would change his life forever. He wanted to get in his pickup truck and just drive, but he didn't. He had no choice but to face the ugly truth about his family. Again.

CHAPTER TWENTY

"I WASN'T THERE that night," Bruce said. "But I know what happened."

Matt was too nervous to sit across from his stepfather. He paced the office, steeling himself for the worst. He briefly thought of the meeting he was going to miss with the electrical contracting company at the job site, but it didn't matter. The entire company might be circling the drain if his worst fears were true. Rescheduling a meeting was a drop in the bucket.

"I always wondered. I'll admit that," Bruce continued. "But I lacked the courage to ask."

Matt stopped pacing and faced the wood-paneled wall instead of his stepfather. Pictures of previous construction jobs were framed and hung there. Certificates of merit. Newspaper articles. Bayside Construction's certificate of operations. The company's wall of fame.

"You should just tell me," he said. His heart was so heavy it couldn't take any more burdens, but he had to. There was no stopping now. He'd seen Caroline's face, and it was clear she had told his stepfather something catastrophic. What would she do with her information?

"JC Construction should never have taken on the massive job of building the Loose Cannon. Back in 1984, my brother had big dreams. He bid the job, but he didn't know what he was doing. He had the winning bid because it was the lowest dollar amount, but it was too low. It forced him to cut corners and save money here and there or he'd lose his shirt on the whole deal."

"Did you know about this at the time?" Matt asked.

Bruce shook his head. "My brother was a proud man. He didn't want to admit it to anyone, even his own flesh and blood. And I wasn't in the construction business then. I wanted to follow my father into banking at that time. Maybe he thought I wouldn't have understood."

Matt thought about his own father's crimes and how he'd never even told his wife. Stubbornness and secrecy were damaging and especially cruel to those closest to a person.

"I heard the whole story for the first time last winter, just a week before John died," Bruce said. He slumped in his chair, his elbows on his desk, hands supporting his head.

Even in the silence of the office, it was hard for Matt to hear his stepfather's words. Perhaps saying them out loud was painful enough. Volume would increase the pain to an unbearable level.

Did his mother know what Bruce now knew about the crime—yes, that was clearly the word—thirty years ago? How would she take the news that she would be facing public ignominy again, and again through no fault of her own?

Matt crossed the room and put a hand on Bruce's back. "I'm sorry," he said. He expected to feel his stepfather's back shaking with sobs, but he only felt the rattling in his chest as he took a deep breath. This was cruel, forcing a story from an ill man, but he had to know the truth.

His relationship with Caroline was beyond

saving now. The pain of that realization cut deep, but Matt put it aside. He couldn't think about it. Not yet.

"My brother wasn't a terrible person. I want you to know that. People do things when their back is against the wall. He wanted to save his company at all costs, but the cost was much higher than he'd ever imagined."

Matt sat in the chair across from Bruce's desk and leaned in so he could hear. Their secretary was at her desk out in the hallway, but the door was closed. Nelma wouldn't hear them unless they raised their voices. Matt felt as if he was in a clandestine meeting, and perhaps he was.

"They cut corners, like I said. Used cheaper material. Less concrete. It was probably a blessing the ride failed right away and they took it down. It would have continued failing if they'd left it in place. Who knows how many people might have been endangered."

"Do you know what caused the accident?" Matt asked.

"Bolts twisted off on part of the structure. They mostly used the right grade of bolts, but there was just the one section where they went cheap. I don't know if they ran out of the grade eights or what happened, but they used fives. You know enough about construction to know what'll happen to lower-grade bolts under stress."

Matt nodded, even though Bruce's eyes were closed and he didn't see his assent.

"Made the track dip and threw the car just enough to toss out a lightweight girl," Bruce continued. "It didn't come off the track, and it was dark, so it wasn't obvious unless you looked closely."

Bruce coughed and rubbed his chest with both hands. Matt went to the mini refrigerator and grabbed a bottle of cold water for his stepfather.

"He knew it would come to light the next day," Bruce continued. "As soon as the sun came up and someone climbed up to take a close look at that part of the ride."

Matt took a deep breath. "So Uncle John went in that night," he said.

Bruce nodded. "With a couple of his trusted guys. They paid off the lone security guard and sneaked in. It couldn't have been easy, but they replaced the bolts on that section of the ride. With no physical evidence, the crew that came in from the state didn't see any specific reason for the accident. They couldn't blame John's company, and no one was the wiser."

Matt thought of the girl who was killed on the ride and whose parents never got answers. Caroline's neighbors who'd lived with the heavy sorrow for thirty years. Had it ever gotten easier for them? Would it help now if they knew what caused the accident?

He was afraid to ask the next question, but he had to. He had to know what happened to the maintenance man whose death was labeled an accident.

"No one from Starlight Point was at the accident scene overnight?" Matt asked.

Bruce steepled his hands and rested his forehead on them. "I didn't want to tell you this, son, but I won't keep the truth from you."

"The maintenance man who was electrocuted," Matt prompted.

"Not an accident." Bruce said, tears running down his cheeks. "It's a hard thing to face, knowing your own brother is a murderer."

He let the terrible word hang in the air for a moment while he dug a handkerchief from his pocket and blew his nose.

"My own brother," he said. "The only thing I can say for him is he didn't plan it. Heat of the moment, I guess. Desperation. He said the guy was going to blow the whistle. John knew he'd be blamed for the girl's death. The problems with the ride would come to light. He'd lose everything."

"No excuse," Matt said.

"I know. I swear to you I never knew this until last winter. I knew John was a changed man after that summer thirty years ago. He lost all the swagger from his step. I tried to talk to him over the years, but he clammed up. I thought it was just the general feeling of failure and having to tear down something he'd just built…you know how it is, son. You build things. Imagine what that'd take out of you."

Matt nodded. It would be terrible, but it was still no excuse to kill.

"So he confessed this to you on his deathbed?"

"Just before." Bruce swiped a hand over his eyes. "Gotta tell you, I wish he'd taken it to his grave instead of burdening me. Maybe I'm a coward for saying that, but I've struggled with it every day since, what to do with this terrible knowledge."

Matt sat in the familiar chair where he and Bruce had talked about the business a hundred times. But everything was different now.

"What are you going to do?" Matt asked.

"It's not up to me anymore," Bruce said quietly. He raised his head and looked Matt in the eye. "The company is yours. I'm handing it all over to you. It's something I've wanted to do since spring, but my brother's secret has been holding me back. I didn't know how I could give you the company without telling you the truth. Now the truth's out, you may not want Bayside Construction, but I'm telling you, it's yours. And you're free to do whatever you have to do."

Matt felt as if the floor had opened up beneath his chair. His dream of taking over the family legacy had come true, but it came with a nightmare attached.

CALLING A MEETING with the police chief at Starlight Point and asking Evie Hamilton to be there was one of the bravest things Caroline had ever done. She was sticking her neck out and risking everything. Her relationship with her sister-in-law. Her job at Starlight Point. Her police chief's respect and potential recommendation for the police academy.

Worst of all, the relationship she and Matt Dunbar had been slowly building all summer. The physical pain squeezing her heart when she thought of what Matt would suffer confirmed what she already knew but had been afraid to admit to herself.

She loved him. Every action, every word, every moment she'd shared with him all summer had led to the most exquisite and agonizing thing she'd ever felt. She just wished she could have told him before it was too late.

But she had no choice now. She'd already taken the first step in destroying any feelings he might have for her. There was no going back now, no matter how much it hurt. No matter who it would hurt.

"I don't have any new evidence," Caroline told Evie and the chief after she'd shared her entire theory. "But I know who to ask. Bruce must know the truth, but he's been silent all these years. Probably because he's guilty."

"This doesn't make sense," Evie protested. "I'm not doubting your powers of investigation and perception, but I can't understand why no one figured this out years ago. If this is true."

They were all in the police chief's office. Evie sat in front of the chief's desk and Caroline leaned on the closed door of his office. As the person in charge of safety at Starlight Point, Evie needed to be in on the conversation. If an old investigation involving the park's police department was going to be reopened, she would be in the middle of it. Smack dab in the middle of a nightmare.

The chief did a slow spiral in his chair. In the two summers Caroline had worked for him, she had seen that stalling technique over and over. It was his way of thinking before speaking.

Evie was apparently aware of his habit as well because she crossed one long leg over the other and waited. Caroline wondered if her brother had shared any of their conversations with his wife. Had he already told Evie about Caroline's summer project investigating the old Loose Cannon incident? Evie couldn't be happy about exposing Starlight Point to an ugly public scandal. Could Starlight Point still be held accountable for the accident and the two deaths after all these years?

Caroline knew the answer to that question. There was no statute of limitations on murder. But the murder, if her theory proved correct, was not on the shoulders of Starlight Point. It was squarely on the construction company. Matt's family.

Her heart tightened in her chest at the thought of the conversation that might be going on at that moment in the downtown office of Bayside Construction, which she'd left only thirty minutes ago.

Were they plotting how to avoid scandal and prosecution? Was Bruce going through files right now and destroying any evidence that might linger after three decades? Caroline wondered if there were construction reports or receipts that would provide evidence of the faulty construction. If so, she was sure that a man who'd gotten away with murder had probably destroyed them.

Was Matt finding out about his family's

crimes for the first time, or had he known all along? The question made her nauseous. She pushed off the door and paced around the office. The chief stopped his slow circuit in his chair and put both hands on the edge of his desk.

"If the bolt issue and the murder never came to light years ago, there was probably a reason. Either the theory has no merit, or somebody wanted to keep it quiet."

Caroline snorted. "Of course somebody wanted to keep it quiet. John Corbin would've lost everything if people knew he cut corners on that ride and caused a death. His brother wasn't going to raise red flags either because he benefited by buying the company. Starlight Point probably wanted the whole thing to go away as fast as possible because of the negative publicity. A no-fault determination from the state investigation and an accidental death label on the maintenance man's death made the whole thing go away."

She'd raised her voice more than she intended and her words were harsh and bitter. It sounded as if she were a judge condemning everyone involved.

Evie let out a long, loud breath. Caroline didn't know how far she was going in destroying her relationship with her sister-in-law, but she couldn't stop now.

"I read the old newspapers at the library," Caroline said in a lower voice. "After two weeks, they didn't even mention the story again. With social media nowadays, people might've talked it up and demanded answers, but at the time it just went away."

Chief Walker gave Caroline a hard look. "You've never told me why this accident is so important to you. There's got to be a reason beyond just your nose for crime."

Caroline crossed her arms over her chest. "I know the family of the girl who was killed. She was only twelve." To her horror, her eyes filled with tears and her voice shook. She did not want to show weakness and emotion in front of her boss, but the girl who was killed and her sister, Catherine, had become linked in her mind throughout the summer.

The police chief's mouth was open and his eyes large. Caroline wondered if he was more shocked that she knew the girl's family or that she had tears flooding her eyes.

Evie didn't look surprised at all. She got up and hugged Caroline.

"I understand," she said quietly as she rubbed Caroline's back.

"You're doing better than I am," the chief said. "What's going on?"

Caroline shook her head, unable to explain without more tears. Evie turned to the chief. "Caroline and Scott had an older sister who died in an accident when she was twelve. A fire at a hotel. The hotel was at fault, but no one was ever held accountable. It's a terrible burden for people to carry… knowing someone they loved is gone and feeling as if there was no justice."

The chief stood. "I'm sorry, Caroline."

She nodded and managed to murmur "thank you" without her voice quivering. She was glad Evie was there to explain. It was Evie who'd helped Scott overcome his guilt about their sister's death.

"So," Evie said. She put her hands on her hips and stared at the ceiling. "What are we going to do?"

"I think we need to ask some questions. Hard questions," Walker said. "And we have to be prepared to either get stonewalling and denials or worse."

"Worse?" Evie asked.

"We could also get the truth," the chief said.

"How can the truth be worse?" Caroline asked.

"Because if and when we find out what really happened thirty years ago, we have to decide what we're going to do with that information," he said. "I know it might seem obvious to you that we'd turn it all over to the local police, recuse ourselves from the investigation and let the full light of the truth do all the damage it can do."

Caroline and Evie stood silently, waiting. The clock ticked loudly on the wall. The outer door of the police station slammed.

"The truth can be ugly. And we have to decide who it would serve to bring it all to the surface," the chief continued. "If we find out that Corbin is a murderer—"

His words were arrested by the office door whipping open. Matt Dunbar filled the door frame.

Caroline's heart expanded and betrayed her at the same time. She wanted to run to him and hold him in her arms until the look of agony on his face disappeared. But she couldn't. The truth was more important than the way she felt.

CHAPTER TWENTY-ONE

MATT GLANCED AROUND the room. Evie Hamilton was white-faced and the police chief was flushed. Matt knew his own skin was heated with passion but he felt cold and empty at the same time. He looked past Evie and the police chief to Caroline.

Her shoulders slumped and her arms hung loosely at her sides. She looked as if she didn't know what to do and felt powerless. He had never seen her look that way before. And there was something else. Her skin was mottled and her eyes glimmered. Had she been crying?

Matt wanted to go to her and hold her in his arms, but he couldn't. A horrible secret stood between them. He knew it was already out in the open, had heard the words "Corbin" and "murderer" when he'd burst through the door.

The chief was the first to react. He approached Matt, pulled the door shut behind him and pointed to an extra chair next to his desk. "Sit down, Dunbar," he said.

His voice was gruff and Matt wished he could turn and run. But there was no running from the truth, from his family's past. The injustice of everything made his throat tight. He wanted to scream in frustration. How could he be so unlucky that he had a father in prison and a stepfamily he'd just learned was guilty of something worse than embezzlement?

He sank into the chair, not sure his legs could hold him up anymore.

"I'm guessing you came here to tell us something," the chief said.

Matt swallowed. He dug deep for the courage to say the words he had to say. He looked at Caroline. Her eyebrows drew together in an expression of pain. Did she feel his pain? Did she already know what he was going to say?

She nodded slightly and it was enough for him to find the words.

"Two things happened this morning," he said. "My stepfather handed over Bayside Construction to me. He'd been considering it for a while, and it's something I've always wanted."

His words were calm and flat. In another situation, he would have expected to hear congratulations from people he knew, worked for, cared about. But there was only silence. They were waiting for the other thing.

"Along with the company came its secrets," Matt said. He put his elbows on his knees. He wore the rough work pants he always wore. Looked down at his work boots. Felt his calloused hands as he put his face in them.

He was a working man. All he wanted was to build things. To build a company and a life he could be proud of. But there was no burying this secret, no matter how much heavy equipment he had at his disposal. He thought of the men working at the construction site only several hundred yards away. They had no idea their lives were about to change, too, when construction came to a stop and they were out of a job.

"Go on," the chief said.

"My uncle, John Corbin, owned JC Construction. They built the Loose Cannon that opened back in 1985. I know you already know that. What you may not know is they did a lousy job. Used inferior materials, cut corners."

He looked up and met Caroline's gaze.

"They used lower-grade bolts on part of the structure that caused it to fail. The accident that killed that girl—" He paused and took a deep breath to steady his voice. "It was JC Construction's fault."

He noticed that both Evie and the chief glanced at Caroline when he admitted this.

"We figured that out," the chief said. "Tell us what happened that night."

Matt leaned back in his chair. His fingers gripped his knees and dug in painfully. "Uncle John knew he'd be blamed, knew he was at fault. He was…desperate. He took a small crew of trusted employees, only two or three I think. Paid off the cop on duty."

Chief Walker nodded, his expression grim. "I always wondered about that—why no one found George Dupont's body until hours later when it was cold."

"They went in and shored up the damaged part," Matt continued. "Replaced the number five bolts with eights. They were able to get away with putting on new parts because the whole ride was still pretty new."

Caroline came closer and leaned on the edge of the chief's desk. She was almost close enough to touch, but he didn't dare. He would lose the fragile grip on his own emotions, and she would probably kill him with her bare hands anyway.

"They got caught, didn't they?" she asked.

Matt nodded. "The head of maintenance suspected. He would've known something about construction and rides, and he probably figured out there was a failure. It was dark, but he was in there with a flashlight checking it out for himself."

"I was a rookie cop here that season," the chief interjected. "I remember stringing yellow tape all around that area before we went off shift. Not that crime tape ever stopped anyone."

"There was an argument. A struggle. I'm not making excuses for my uncle, I'm not. But he had everything on the line." Matt looked Caroline right in the eye and said the hardest thing. "My uncle shoved that maintenance man into the electrical panel and killed him so he wouldn't blow the whistle."

Silence hung over the office for a moment. Matt wished he could fix everything. He could build a complicated structure from only a drawing, but he could see no way out of this.

"That's the theory Caroline came up with," the chief said. "But what I'd like to know is how you know this whole story. Was Bruce Corbin there that night?"

"No," Matt roared. He came out of his chair and the chief and Evie took a step back. Caroline didn't budge. He held up both hands in a conciliatory gesture. "No," he repeated more calmly. "My stepfather didn't know about the faulty construction or the murder until this past winter. My uncle told him right before he died. I guess he didn't want to die with that stain on his conscience, but it's pretty damn hard for my stepfather to live knowing it."

"And now we all know it," Caroline said quietly.

"Do you believe your stepfather?" the chief asked. "Believe him when he says he wasn't involved and didn't know?"

Matt remembered the grave change that had come over Bruce Corbin last winter. He remembered Bruce's grief at his brother's death, and his far greater grief as he revealed the ugly story just an hour ago.

"I do," Matt said. He looked back at Caroline. "I have to believe him. He doesn't have much time left, and he's gone downhill fast since the time of John's death. I know my stepfather. He's not the kind of man who would live a lie all these years."

Matt thought of his father in prison. Had he not been a child, would he have suspected or known of his father's crimes? Was he a good judge of character, or was he easily fooled when he wanted to believe in someone?

"I'm going to ask you to step outside, but don't leave," the chief said. "We're going to talk about this."

"Let him stay," Caroline said. "There's nothing we can say that he doesn't already know."

CAROLINE WAITED FOR the police chief or Evie to speak first. Although she was the one who'd opened the investigation and caused the truth to come out after decades of deceit, she wasn't in charge now. Evie owned

Starlight Point. Chief Walker had jurisdiction over police matters.

If it were up to her, what would she do? She tried to remove her feelings from the situation. Tried to isolate her love for Matt from the fact that his family business—a business he now controlled—had been involved in the worst possible crime. The worst betrayal.

But that betrayal wasn't Matt's. And, in fact, there was no one left alive to charge with the crime. A dead man couldn't be prosecuted. A defunct, sold and renamed company couldn't be blamed or even sued.

The case was dead in the water.

She waited for Evie or the chief to speak, but they didn't. They were looking at her.

"We have answers," she said. "That's what I wanted when I started this. I wanted answers about that girl's death. I wanted to be able to go to her parents and tell them what happened."

"Will that make them feel better?" Evie asked.

Caroline tried to imagine a scene in which she told them shoddy construction had taken their daughter, but there was no one left to blame. Would their eyes light up with joy knowing why their daughter died? She pictured their empty faces instead. What good would it really do?

She shook her head. "No," she said. "Knowing who to blame won't bring back their daughter. She's at peace in her grave. Her parents have had a long time to accept that."

She crossed to the window and looked outside. She didn't want anyone to see her face right now because she knew it would reveal a lifetime of sorrow and grief for the sister she never knew. Nothing would bring her back, either.

Caroline's body was so tight she was afraid she would break. Tears raced down her cheeks and she tried not to shake or sob so no one would know she was crying. It was such a relief, letting the grief out. Was this what she'd waited for all these years? A chance to realize that blaming someone and seeking justice wouldn't make any difference?

But it had made a difference for her. Caroline watched a bird fly past the window and flap its wings, staying steady in a summer breeze.

This journey had brought her peace. She suddenly realized that's what she'd wanted all along. Catherine was also at peace in her grave. Caroline's parents had accepted it. Scott had accepted it. It was her turn.

She realized she was sobbing openly now. She heard steps behind her and felt strong arms enclosing her. Matt's lips brushed her temple.

"I'm sorry," he whispered.

"Don't be," she said. She turned into his embrace, slid her arms around him and rested her cheek on his hard chest. She wished she could stay like that forever, but it was over. She'd nearly destroyed Matt by pursuing her case. She would emerge with a lightened heart, but he wouldn't. He'd finally gotten what he wanted, the company. But it was tainted now. He'd inherited another mess.

"What happens next?" Evie asked.

Caroline pulled her cheek from Matt's chest and stepped back. If she didn't let go now, she was afraid she wouldn't be able to. She squared her shoulders.

"Criminally," she said, addressing her words to her police chief, "I think we have no case. There's no more physical evidence now than there was thirty years ago."

"Are you sure about that?"

"All you have is my hunch about what happened."

"That's not true," Matt said. "I'm not covering this up. You have to go forward with the case."

"What case?" Caroline asked. "We can't charge a dead man with a murder. We can't charge his brother for concealing evidence when he didn't even know about it for thirty years. There is no case."

"But what about the man who was murdered? Doesn't he deserve justice?"

Caroline thought about that man. His terrible last moments. She'd read his file, knew he was a dedicated employee, a hardworking man who loved Starlight Point. He'd died trying to defend the place he worked. The man had no family other than his mother who had passed away years ago. There was no family to bring justice to, and the truth would destroy another family.

She thought of Lucas and Matt's mother.

What would happen to them if Bayside Construction were dragged through the mud?

"He does deserve justice," Caroline said. "He deserves for someone to know how he died."

"We know," Evie said, her voice shaking with emotion. "We know his story. The three of us."

Caroline nodded. "It's enough. It's all we have."

Matt turned to Evie. "I'm sure you don't want my family building your new ride now. I'll resign the contract and do everything I can to help the transition to a new builder."

"You can't do that," Evie said. "We've already made payments. You signed a contract."

"I'll find a way to repay you," he said.

Before Evie could argue, Matt spun around and abruptly left.

Evie, the chief and Caroline stared at each other for a moment and then the chief walked over and closed his office door.

"What we heard today stays in this office. There's no reason to file any charges, and no reason to hurt anyone by making it public. As far as I'm concerned, the Loose Cannon is put to rest for good."

Evie lifted sympathetic eyes to Caroline. "Are you okay with this? I don't want you to feel as if we're covering up what you found."

Caroline took a long breath and let it out.

"We're not," she said. "The past is already buried. Believe it or not, I found something else this summer—something I wasn't even looking for."

Evie smiled. "Well then, I wish you'd go after Matt and tell him, from me, that he's not fired. I want that new ride done on time just as we hired him to do. You can add whatever you want and tell him in whatever way you think will be most convincing."

The police chief laughed and tried to cover it with a cough.

If I go after him, what will I say? What will he say? Caroline wished she could run Matt down and hold him in her arms until everything else disappeared. What would he do? Did he love her as much as she loved him? Would love be enough to erase the scars from both their pasts?

No matter the risk, she was going to try.

"You're the boss," she said as she dashed out of the office.

She ran across the midway from the corporate office to the construction zone. She passed honking and flashing Kiddie Land rides, her feet flashing on the white concrete reflecting the morning sun. Each step felt lighter than the last.

Was she selling out by giving up an old investigation? No one had asked her to dig around in the bones from the past. More important, no one would be served by knowing the facts of the case after thirty years. No one's burden would be lightened. Not even hers. She'd found a different way to shed the heavy weight she'd been carrying.

She caught up with Matt just as he was about to go through the locked gate on the midway side of the construction zone. The gate was largely concealed by an old cottonwood tree, and Matt was shoving his key into the padlock. Sunlight glinted off his blond hair.

"You can't go in there," Caroline said as she raced up behind him.

Matt turned. His shoulders slumped with defeat and his face was grim.

"I suppose you have to escort me off the property," he said. He held her eyes for a moment and then dropped his glance to the pavement.

"Hold out your hands," Caroline said.

Matt hesitated and then held them both out as if he expected her to cuff him.

Caroline wanted to laugh at his resigned expression, but she couldn't. She was the one who had brought him to this. She stepped closer, took both his hands and raised up on her toes to kiss him. His eyes opened wide with astonishment as he kissed her back.

"You can't go in there because you don't have your hard hat," she said. "It's not safe."

She released his hands and ran her fingers through his short hair. He closed his eyes as she massaged his scalp. "I don't deserve this," he said. "I don't deserve someone as wonderful as you being so nice to me."

He slid his arms around her and kissed her cheek. "But I'll take it," he whispered in her ear. "If only for another moment."

She pulled back and frowned. "What have you done wrong?" she asked. "Nothing. It's not your fault there seem to be criminal tendencies in your family one generation back.

Those are not your flaws and you can't fix them, no matter how good you are at building things."

"I wish I could. Wish I could bring back the people who were harmed, erase it all."

"You can't change the past," Caroline said. "I've seen your true colors this summer, Matt. I know you're going to be okay. You're going to be great at running this business."

He shook his head. "I can't. I can't take over a business that's built on a lie."

Caroline poked him in the chest with one finger. "Haven't you been paying attention today? The truth came to light at the very moment you took over. That's what you're building on."

Matt's mouth dropped open. He turned and glanced up at the steel beams that already towered over the fence. A small smile creased his face.

"I hadn't thought of it that way."

"That's what you need me for," Caroline said.

Matt returned his attention to her. "I do need you."

"Good."

"Caroline, I don't know if you feel the same way, but I've been falling in love with you little by little all summer."

Caroline touched his cheek. "Last week when you told me that even if I didn't want to be with you, you'd still watch for me around every corner... I can't stop thinking about that. Because it's exactly how I feel about you. As I've stood outside this fence, I've thought about what you were doing on the other side. Everything that's happened this summer, I always thought about how you were feeling about it. Do you know what this means?"

"I think it means what I hope it does."

"It means I love you, too."

Matt smiled and kissed Caroline. The old-fashioned steam train gave a long, low whistle, but Caroline hardly noticed it. All her senses were wrapped up in the man she hadn't been able to take her mind off of since she'd met him.

The gate next to them rattled and opened from the inside and one of Matt's men leaned out.

"Dunbar, where you been all morning?"

When the construction worker realized

what was going on, he quickly looked away and put his hands in his pockets.

"I've been busy," Matt said.

"Well, could you get un-busy? I'm trying to stall off those electrical contractors, but they're starting to get grouchy. I was just going to run down the midway and get some doughnuts. Thought it might distract 'em until we could figure out where the heck you were."

Matt laughed. "Tell you what, we'll go get the doughnuts. Tell those contractors to cool their heels for a few more minutes. We've got all summer."

The worker shook his head, grinning in disbelief. He ducked back through the gate and closed it behind him.

Matt took Caroline's hand. "Want to take a walk down the midway with me? We have a lot of talking to do."

"One more kiss first," Caroline said.

The old-fashioned cars honked on the track nearby and riders screamed merrily on the scrambler ride across the midway while Caroline and Matt kissed in the sunshine at Starlight Point.

EPILOGUE

THE DAY BEFORE Starlight Point opened its gates to thousands of excited guests and roller coaster fans was a special beginning of another kind. Caroline's heart fluttered, and she saw her own anticipation and joy reflected on her groom's face. The spring breeze blew her short ivory veil across her eyes, blurring her vision. She was glad she'd allowed her mother to talk her into a few sparkly sequins on the veil, which caught the sunlight and added to the thrill of the occasion.

Matt reached up and pushed the veil back gently, just enough so he could lean in for a ceremonial kiss when the minister gave his official blessing.

"I never thought I'd be standing here," he whispered.

"You didn't believe you'd get this roller coaster built on time?" Caroline asked.

"I never believed I'd be standing here with the woman I love," Matt said. He touched her cheek. "I still don't know how I got this lucky, but I promise to spend the rest of my life making you glad you said yes to me."

"You don't have to do that," Caroline said. "I'm already glad. I love you, Matt."

They stood on the platform of the Super Star roller coaster, which had been completed on time and was even more beautifully complex than Caroline imagined. Twisted in entangled loops with the Shooting Star, the new ride was already getting rave reviews from advance riders and the media.

Caroline knew Matt wished his stepfather were alive to see the new ride open, but Matt took comfort knowing the ride's success ensured the future of a company and a family Bruce had loved.

The Hamiltons mingled with Matt's and Caroline's families and other guests as they celebrated on the platform of the ride that had brought Matt and Caroline together. Matt's entire crew, including Jackson—who had recovered from the accident on the site—was there wearing ties instead of hard hats.

Matt kissed Caroline again, his lips lingering on hers until his brother and best man cleared his throat.

"It's time," Lucas announced.

A sleek black and white train slid into the platform loading area and the lap bars released.

"Everybody on!" Jack Hamilton said.

The entire wedding party climbed into the seats, tucking dresses and suit jackets in around them. They buckled up, pulled down their lap bars and headed out of the station.

Matt and Caroline had the first seat as they ascended the tall hill to celebrate the official beginning of their lives together. They held hands the entire time, knowing the ride would be much more fun because they were together.

* * * * *

*Don't miss the next book
in Amie Denman's*
STARLIGHT POINT STORIES
*miniseries, coming March 2018
from Harlequin Heartwarming.*

*And check out previous books
in the miniseries:*

*UNDER THE BOARDWALK
CAROUSEL NIGHTS
MEET ME ON THE MIDWAY*

Get 2 Free Books,
Plus 2 Free Gifts—
just for trying the Reader Service!

Love Inspired®

YES! Please send me 2 FREE Love Inspired® Romance novels and my 2 FREE mystery gifts (gifts are worth about $10 retail). After receiving them, if I don't wish to receive any more books, I can return the shipping statement marked "cancel." If I don't cancel, I will receive 6 brand-new novels every month and be billed just $5.24 for the regular-print edition or $5.74 each for the larger-print edition in the U.S., or $5.74 each for the regular-print edition or $6.24 each for the larger-print edition in Canada. That's a saving of at least 13% off the cover price. It's quite a bargain! Shipping and handling is just 50¢ per book in the U.S. and 75¢ per book in Canada.* I understand that accepting the 2 free books and gifts places me under no obligation to buy anything. I can always return a shipment and cancel at any time. The free books and gifts are mine to keep no matter what I decide.

Please check one:
☐ Love Inspired Romance Regular-Print   ☐ Love Inspired Romance Larger-Print
(105/305 IDN GLWW)   (122/322 IDN GLWW)

Name	(PLEASE PRINT)

Address	Apt. #

City	State/Province	Zip/Postal Code

Signature (if under 18, a parent or guardian must sign)

Mail to the **Reader Service:**
IN U.S.A.: P.O. Box 1341, Buffalo, NY 14240-8531
IN CANADA: P.O. Box 603, Fort Erie, Ontario L2A 5X3

Want to try two free books from another line?
Call 1-800-873-8635 today or visit www.ReaderService.com.

*Terms and prices subject to change without notice. Prices do not include applicable taxes. Sales tax applicable in N.Y. Canadian residents will be charged applicable taxes. Offer not valid in Quebec. This offer is limited to one order per household. Books received may not be as shown. Not valid for current subscribers to Love Inspired Romance books. All orders subject to approval. Credit or debit balances in a customer's account(s) may be offset by any other outstanding balance owed by or to the customer. Please allow 4 to 6 weeks for delivery. Offer available while quantities last.

Your Privacy—The Reader Service is committed to protecting your privacy. Our Privacy Policy is available online at www.ReaderService.com or upon request from the Reader Service.

We make a portion of our mailing list available to reputable third parties that offer products we believe may interest you. If you prefer that we not exchange your name with third parties, or if you wish to clarify or modify your communication preferences, please visit us at www.ReaderService.com/consumerschoice or write to us at Reader Service Preference Service, P.O. Box 9062, Buffalo, NY 14240-9062. Include your complete name and address.

LI17R2

Get 2 Free Books,

Plus 2 Free Gifts—

just for trying the Reader Service!

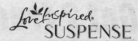

YES! Please send me 2 FREE Love Inspired® Suspense novels and my 2 FREE mystery gifts (gifts are worth about $10 retail). After receiving them, if I don't wish to receive any more books, I can return the shipping statement marked "cancel." If I don't cancel, I will receive 4 brand-new novels every month and be billed just $5.24 each for the regular-print edition or $5.74 each for the larger-print edition in the U.S., or $5.74 each for the regular-print edition or $6.24 each for the larger-print edition in Canada. That's a savings of at least 13% off the cover price. It's quite a bargain! Shipping and handling is just 50¢ per book in the U.S. and 75¢ per book in Canada.* I understand that accepting the 2 free books and gifts places me under no obligation to buy anything. I can always return a shipment and cancel at any time. The free books and gifts are mine to keep no matter what I decide.

Please check one: ☐ Love Inspired Suspense Regular-Print   ☐ Love Inspired Suspense Larger-Print
                               (153/353 IDN GLW2)   (107/307 IDN GLW2)

Name _____ (PLEASE PRINT) _____

Address _____ Apt. #

City _____ State/Prov. _____ Zip/Postal Code

Signature (if under 18, a parent or guardian must sign)

Mail to the **Reader Service:**
IN U.S.A.: P.O. Box 1341, Buffalo, NY 14240-8531
IN CANADA: P.O. Box 603, Fort Erie, Ontario L2A 5X3

Want to try two free books from another line?
Call 1-800-873-8635 or visit www.ReaderService.com.

* Terms and prices subject to change without notice. Prices do not include applicable taxes. Sales tax applicable in N.Y. Canadian residents will be charged applicable taxes. Offer not valid in Quebec. This offer is limited to one order per household. Books received may not be as shown. Not valid for current subscribers to Love Inspired Suspense books. All orders subject to approval. Credit or debit balances in a customer's account(s) may be offset by any other outstanding balance owed by or to the customer. Please allow 4 to 6 weeks for delivery. Offer available while quantities last.

Your Privacy—The Reader Service is committed to protecting your privacy. Our Privacy Policy is available online at www.ReaderService.com or upon request from the Reader Service.

We make a portion of our mailing list available to reputable third parties that offer products we believe may interest you. If you prefer that we not exchange your name with third parties, or if you wish to clarify or modify your communication preferences, please visit us at www.ReaderService.com/consumerschoice or write to us at Reader Service Preference Service, P.O. Box 9062, Buffalo, NY 14240-9062. Include your complete name and address.

LIS17R2

HOMETOWN HEARTS ♡

YES! Please send me **The Hometown Hearts Collection** in Larger Print. This collection begins with 3 FREE books and 2 FREE gifts in the first shipment. Along with my 3 free books, I'll also get the next 4 books from the Hometown Hearts Collection, in LARGER PRINT, which I may either return and owe nothing, or keep for the low price of $4.99 U.S./ $5.89 CDN each plus $2.99 for shipping and handling per shipment*. If I decide to continue, about once a month for 8 months I will get 6 or 7 more books, but will only need to pay for 4. That means 2 or 3 books in every shipment will be FREE! If I decide to keep the entire collection, I'll have paid for only 32 books because 19 books are FREE! I understand that accepting the 3 free books and gifts places me under no obligation to buy anything. I can always return a shipment and cancel at any time. My free books and gifts are mine to keep no matter what I decide.

262 HCN 3432 462 HCN 3432

Name	(PLEASE PRINT)	
Address		Apt. #
City	State/Prov.	Zip/Postal Code

Signature (if under 18, a parent or guardian must sign)

Mail to the **Reader Service:**

IN U.S.A.: P.O. Box 1867, Buffalo, NY. 14240-1867
IN CANADA: P.O. Box 609, Fort Erie, Ontario L2A 5X3

* Terms and prices subject to change without notice. Prices do not include applicable taxes. Sales tax applicable in NY. Canadian residents will be charged applicable taxes. This offer is limited to one order per household. All orders subject to approval. Credit or debit balances in a customer's account(s) may be offset by any other outstanding balance owed by or to the customer. Please allow 4 to 6 weeks for delivery. Offer available while quantities last. Offer not available to Quebec residents.

Your Privacy—The Reader Service is committed to protecting your privacy. Our Privacy Policy is available online at www.ReaderService.com or upon request from the Reader Service.

We make a portion of our mailing list available to reputable third parties that offer products we believe may interest you. If you prefer that we not exchange your name with third parties, or if you wish to clarify or modify your communication preferences, please visit us at www.ReaderService.com/consumerschoice or write to us at Reader Service Preference Service, P.O. Box 9062, Buffalo, NY. 14240-9062. Include your complete name and address.

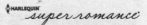

READERSERVICE.COM

Manage your account online!

- Review your order history
- Manage your payments
- Update your address

We've designed the Reader Service website just for you.

Enjoy all the features!

- Discover new series available to you, and read excerpts from any series.
- Respond to mailings and special monthly offers.
- Browse the Bonus Bucks catalog and online-only exculsives.
- Share your feedback.

Visit us at:

ReaderService.com